THOMAS M. DISCH

THE GENOCIDES

Thomas M. Disch is the author of numerous novels, story collections, books of poetry, criticism, children's literature, libretti, and plays.

THE GENOCIDES

THE GENOCIDES

THOMAS M. DISCH

VINTAGE BOOKS

A DIVISION OF RANDOM HOUSE, INC.

NEW YORK

FIRST VINTAGE BOOKS EDITION, NOVEMBER 2000

Copyright © 1965, copyright renewed 1993
by Thomas M. Disch

Library of Congress Cataloging-in-Publication Data
Disch, Thomas M.
The Genocides / Thomas M. Disch— 1st Vintage Books ed.
p.   cm.
ISBN 978-0-375-70546-5
1. Plants—Fiction. I. Science fiction.
PS3554.18 G46 2000
813'.54—dc21   00-042339

www.vintagebooks.com

146119709

The harvest is past, the summer is ended,

and we are not saved.

Jeremiah 8:20

CONTENTS

THE GENOCIDES

ONE THE PRODIGAL

As the lesser and then the greater stars disappeared in the advancing light, the towering mass of the forest that walled in the cornfield retained for a while the utter blackness of the night. A light breeze blew in from the lake, rustling the leaves of the young corn, but the leaves of that dark forest did not stir. Now the eastern forest wall glowed gray-green, and the three men waiting in the field knew, though they could not yet see it, that the sun was up.

Anderson spat—the day's work had officially begun. He began to make his way up the gentle incline toward the eastern forest wall. Four rows away on either side of him, his sons followed—Neil, the younger and larger, on his right hand, and Buddy on the left.

Each man carried two empty wooden buckets. None wore either shoes or shirts, for it was midsummer. Their denims were in tatters. Anderson and Buddy had on wide-brimmed hats woven of crude raffia, like the coolie hats you used to get at carnivals and state fairs. Neil had sunglasses but no hat. They were old; the bridge had been broken and mended with glue and a strip of that same fiber from which the hats had been made. His nose was calloused where the glasses rested.

Buddy was the last to reach the top of the hill. His father smiled while he waited for him to catch up. Anderson's smile was never a good sign.

"You're sore from yesterday?"

"I'm fine. The stiffness comes out when I get working."

Neil laughed. "Buddy's sore because he *has* to work. Ain't that so, Buddy?"

It was a joke. But Anderson, whose style it was to be laconic, never laughed at jokes, and Buddy rarely found very funny the jokes his half-brother made.

"Don't you get it?" Neil asked. "*Sore.* Buddy's *sore* because he has to work."

"We all have to work," Anderson said, and that pretty well ended what joke there had been.

They began to work.

Buddy withdrew a plug from his tree and inserted a metal tube where the plug had been. Below the makeshift spigot he hung one of the buckets. Pulling the plugs was hard work, for they had been in place a week and had stuck fast. The sap, drying about the plug, acted as a glue. This work seemed always to last just long enough for the soreness—of his fingers, his wrists, his arms, his back—to reassert itself, but never to abate.

Before the terrible work of carrying the buckets began, Buddy stopped and stared at the sap trickling through the pipe and oozing, like lime-green honey, into the bucket. It was coming out slowly today. By the end of the summer this tree would be dying and ready to be cut down.

Seen up close, it didn't seem much like a tree at all. Its skin was smooth, like the stem of a flower. A proper tree this size would have split through its skin under the pressure of its own growth, and its trunk would be rough with bark. Farther back in the forest, you could find trees, big ones, which had reached the limit of their growth and begun at last to form something like bark. At least their trunks, though green, weren't moist to the touch like this one. Those trees—or Plants, as Anderson called them—were six hundred feet tall, and their biggest leaves were the size of billboards. Here on the edge of the cornfield the growth was more recent—not more than two years—and the highest stood only a hundred and fifty feet tall. Even so, here as deeper in the forest, the sun came through the foliage at noonday as pale as moon-light on a clouded night.

"Get the lead out!" Anderson called. He was already out in the field with his full buckets of sap, and the sap was brimming over Buddy's buckets too. *Why is there never time to think?* Buddy envied Neil's mulish capacity just to *do* things, to spin the wheel of his cage without wondering overmuch how it worked.

"Right away!" Neil yelled from a distance.

"Right away!" Buddy echoed, thankful his half-brother too had been caught up in his own thoughts, whatever they could be.

Of the three men working in the field, Neil surely had the best body. Except for a receding chin that gave a false impression of weakness, he was strong and well proportioned. He was a good six inches taller than his father or Buddy, both short men. His shoulders were broader, his chest thicker, and his muscles, though not so well knit as Anderson's, were bigger. There was, however, no economy in his movements. When he walked, he lumbered. When he stood, he slouched. He endured the strain of the day's labor better than Buddy simply because he had more material to endure with. In this he was brutish, but worse than being brutish, Neil was dumb, and worse than being dumb, he was mean.

He is mean, Buddy thought, *and he is dangerous.* Buddy set off down the row of corn, a full bucket of sap in either hand and his heart brimming with ill-will. It gave him a sort of strength, and he needed all the strength he could muster, from whatever source. His breakfast had been light, and lunch, he knew, wouldn't be quite enough, and there'd be no dinner to speak of.

Even hunger, he had learned, provided its own kind of strength: the will to wrest more food from the soil and more soil from the Plants.

No matter how much care he took, the sap splattered his pants legs as he walked, and the tattered fabric stuck to his calf. Later, when the day was hotter, his whole body would be covered with sap. The sap would bake dry, and when he moved, the stiffened cloth would tear out the crusted hairs of his body, one by one. The worst of that was over now, thank heaven—the body has a finite number of hairs—but there were still the flies that swarmed over his flesh to feed on the sap. He hated the flies, which did not seem to be finite.

When he reached the foot of the decline and was in the middle of the field, Buddy set one bucket down and began to feed the thirsty young plants from the other. Each plant received about a pound of thick green nutrient—and to good effect. It wasn't the Fourth yet, and already many plants were up over his knees. Corn would have grown well in the rich lake-bottom soil in any case, but with the additional nourishment they drew from the stolen sap, the plants throve phenomenally—as though they were in central Iowa instead of northern Minnesota. This unwitting parasitism of the corn served another purpose besides, for as the corn throve, the Plants whose sap they had drunk died, and each year the limit of the field could be pushed a bit farther.

It had been Anderson's idea to pit the Plant against itself this way, and every corn plant in the field was a testimony to his judgment. Looking down the long rows, the old man felt like a prophet in full view of his prophecy. His regret now was that he hadn't thought of it sooner—before the diaspora of his village, before the Plants had vanquished his and his neighbors' farms.

If only . . .

But that was history, water under the bridge, spilt milk, and as such it belonged to a winter evening in the common-room when there was time for idle regrets. Now, and for the rest of that long day, there was work to do.

Anderson looked about for his sons. They were straggling behind, still emptying their second buckets over the roots of the corn.

"Get the lead out!" he yelled. Then, turning back up the hill with his two buckets empty, he smiled a thin, joyless smile, the smile of a prophet, and spat out, through the gap between his front teeth, a thin stream of the juice of the Plant that he had been chewing.

He hated the Plants, and that hatred gave him strength.

They worked, sweating in the sun, till noonday. Buddy's legs were trembling from the strain and from hunger. But each trip down the rows of corn was shorter, and when he returned to the Plant there was a moment (and each a little longer than the last) before the buckets filled, when he could rest.

Sometimes, though he did not like the vaguely aniselike taste, he would stick his finger into the bucket and lick off the bittersweet syrup. It did not nourish, but it allayed for a while the worst of his hunger. He might have chewed the pulp carved from the phloem of the trunk, as his father and Neil did, but "chewing" reminded him of the life he had tried to escape ten years before, when he had left the farm for the city. His escape had failed, as surely as the cities themselves had failed. At last, just as in the parable, he would have been content with the husks the swine ate, and he had returned to Tassel and to his father's farm.

True to form, the fatted calf had been killed, and if his return had been a parable, it would have ended happily. But it was his life, and he was still, in his heart, a prodigal, and there were times when he wished he had died during the famine of the cities.

But in a contest between the belly's hunger and the mind's variable predilections, the belly is likelier to win. The prodigal's rebellion had been reduced to catchwords and petty crochets: an obstinate refusal to use the word *ain't,* an abiding contempt for country music, a distaste for "chewing," and a loathing for the hick, the hayseed, and the dumb cluck. In a word, for Neil.

The heat and his body's weariness conspired to direct his thoughts to less troubled channels, and as he stood gazing into the slowly filling buckets, his mind surged with the remembered images of other times. Of Babylon, that great city.

He remembered how at night the streets would be swift-flowing rivers of light and how the brilliant, antiseptic cars had streamed down those rivers. From hour to hour the sound would not abate nor the lights dim. There had been the drive-ins, and when there was less money, the White Castles. Girls in shorts waited on your car. Sometimes the shorts were edged with little, glittering fringes that bounced on tan thighs.

In the summer, when the hicks had worked on the farms, there had been flood-lit beaches, and his parched tongue curled now remembering how—in the labyrinth of empty oil drums supporting the diving raft—he would have kissed Irene. Or someone. The names didn't matter so much any more.

He made another trip down the row, and while he fed the corn he remembered the names that didn't matter now. Oh, the city had swarmed with girls. You could stand on a street corner, and in an hour hundreds would walk past. There had even been talk about a population problem then.

Hundreds of thousands of people!

He remembered the crowds in the winter in the heated auditorium on the university campus. He would have come there in a white shirt. The collar would be tight around his neck. In his imagination, he fingered the knot of a silk tie. Would it be striped or plain? He thought of the stores full of suits and jackets. Oh, the colors there had been! the music, and, afterward, the applause!

But the worst of it, he thought, resting by the Plant again, *is that there isn't anyone to talk to any more.* The total population of Tassel was two hundred and forty-seven, and none of them, not one of them, could understand Buddy Anderson. A world had been lost, and they weren't aware of it. It had never been their world, but it had been, briefly, Buddy's, and it had been beautiful.

The buckets were full, and Buddy grabbed hold of the handles and made his way back to the field. For the hundredth time that day, he stepped over the cankerous knob of tissue that had formed on the stump of the Plant that had irrigated these rows last year. This time his bare foot came down on a patch of the slick wood where there was a puddle of slippery sap. Weighted down by the buckets, he couldn't recover his balance. He fell backward, the sap in the buckets spilling out over him. He lay in the dirt, and the sap spread across his chest and down his arms, and the myriad flies settled to feed.

He didn't try to get up.

"Well, don't just *lay* there," Anderson said. "There's work to do." He stretched out a hand, kinder than his words, to help Buddy up.

When he thanked his father, there was a just-perceptible quaver in his voice.

"You all right?"

"I guess so." He felt his coccyx, which had struck against a knob of the stump, and winced.

"Then go down to the stream and wash that crap off. We're about ready to go and eat anyhow."

Buddy nodded. Grabbing the buckets (it was amazing how automatic the work had become, even for him), he set off down a forest path that led to the stream (once, farther inland, it had been Gooseberry River) from which the village drew its water. Seven years ago, this whole area—fields, forest and village—had been under ten to fifteen feet of water. But the Plants had siphoned off the water. They were still at it, and every day the North Shore of Lake Superior moved a few inches farther south, though the rate of its retreat seemed to be lessening, as all but the newest of the Plants reached the limits of their growth.

He stripped and lay down full length in the stream. The tepid water moved languidly over his bare limbs, washing away sap and dirt and the dead flies that had caught on him as on flypaper. He held his breath and lowered his head slowly into the flowing water until he was totally submerged.

With the water in his ears, he could hear slight sounds more distinctly: his back scratching against the pebbles in the bed of the stream, and, more distantly, another sound, a low rumbling that grew, too quickly, to a pounding. He knew the sound, and knew he shouldn't be hearing it now, here.

He lifted his head out of the water in time to see the cow running full-tilt toward him—and in time for her to see him. Gracie jumped, and her hind hooves came down within inches of his thigh. Then she ran on into the forest.

More followed. Buddy counted them as they splashed across the stream: eight . . . eleven . . . twelve. Seven Herefords and five Guernseys. All of them.

The yearning bellow of a bull sounded in the air, and Studs came into view—the village's great, brown Hereford, with his flaring white topknot. He stared at Buddy with casual defiance, but there was more urgent business than the settling of old scores. He hurried on after the cows.

That Studs had gotten out of his pen was bad news, for the cows were all of them half-gone with calves, and it would do them no good to be mounted by an eager bull. The news would be even worse for Neil, who was responsible for Studs. It could mean a whipping. This was not a thought to sadden Buddy deeply, but still he was concerned for the cattle. He hurried into his overalls, which were still sticky with sap.

Before he'd gotten the straps over his shoulders, Jimmie Lee, the younger of Buddy's two half-brothers, came running out of the forest on the bull's trail. His face was flushed with the excitement of the chase, and even as he announced the calamity—"Studs broke out!"—a smile touched his lips.

All children—and Jimmie was no exception—feel a demonic sympathy with those things that cause disorder in the grown-up world. The young thrive on earthquakes, tornadoes and escaped bulls.

It would not do, Buddy realized, to let their father see that smile. For in Anderson the secret sympathy for the powers of destruction had been metamorphosed by the agency of time into a stern, humorless opposition to those same powers, a magnificent, raw willfulness as ruthless in its way as the enemy it opposed. Nothing could more surely elicit that ruthlessness than seeing this hectic flush in the cheeks of his youngest and (it was commonly supposed) dearest.

"I'll tell Father," Buddy said. "You go on after Studs. Where's everyone else?"

"Clay's getting together all the men he can find, and Lady and Blossom and the women are going out to scare the cows away from the corn if they go that way." Jimmie shouted the information over his shoulder as he trotted along the broad trail blazed by the herd.

He was a good boy, Jimmie Lee, and bright as a button. In the old world, Buddy was sure, he would have become another prodigal. It was always the bright one who rebelled. Now he'd be lucky to survive. They all would.

The morning's work accomplished, Anderson looked across his field and saw that it was good. At harvest the ears would not be large and juicy, as in the old times. They had left the bags of hybridized seed moldering in the abandoned storerooms of old Tassel. Hybrids gave the best yield, but they were sterile. Agriculture could no longer afford such fripperies. The variety he was using now was much closer hereditarily to the ancient Indian maize, the Aztec *zea mays*. His whole strategy against the usurping Plants was based on corn. Corn had become the life of his people: it was the bread they ate and the meat as well. In the summer Studs and his twelve wives might get along on the tender green roughage the children scraped from the sides of the Plants or they might graze among the seedlings along the lake shore, but when winter came corn sustained the cattle just as it sustained the villagers.

Corn took care of itself almost as well as it took care of the others. It did not need a plowman to turn over the soil, only a sharp stick to scratch it and hands to drop in the four seeds and the lump of excrement that would be their first food. Nothing gave the yield per acre that corn did; nothing but rice gave as much nourishment per ounce. Land was at a premium now. The Plants exerted a constant pressure on the cornfields. Every day, the smaller children had to go out and hunt between the rows of corn for the lime-green shoots, which could grow in a week's time to the size of saplings, and in a month would be big as grown maples.

Damn them! he thought. *May God damn them!* But this curse lost much of its forcefulness from the conviction that God had sent them in the first place. Let others talk about Outer Space as much as they liked: Anderson knew that the same angry and jealous God who had once before visited a flood upon an earth that was corrupt had created the Plants and sown them. He never argued about it. When God could be so persuasive, why should Anderson raise his voice? It had been seven years that spring since the first seedlings of the Plant had been seen. They had come of a sudden in April of '72, a billion spores, invisible to all but the most powerful microscopes, sown broadcast over the entire planet by an equally invisible sower (and where was the microscope or telescope or radar screen that will make God visible?), and within days every inch of ground, farmland and desert, jungle and tundra, was covered with a carpet of the richest green.

Every year since, as there were fewer and fewer people, there were more converts to Anderson's thesis. Like Noah, he was having the last laugh. But that didn't stop him from hating, just as Noah must have hated the rains and rising waters.

Anderson hadn't always hated the Plants so much. In the first years, when the Government had just toppled and the farms were in their heyday, he had gone out in the moonlight and just watched them grow. It was like the speeded-up movies of plant growth he'd seen in Ag School years ago. He had thought then that he could hold his own against them, but he'd been wrong. The infernal weeds had wrested his farm from his hands and the town from the hands of his people.

But, by God, he'd win it back. Every square inch. If he had to root out every Plant with his two bare hands. He spat significantly.

At such moments Anderson was as conscious of his own strength, of the force of his resolve, as a young man is conscious of the compulsion of his flesh or a woman is conscious of the child she bears. It was an animal strength, and that, Anderson knew, was the only strength strong enough to prevail against the Plants.

His oldest son ran out of the forest shouting. When Buddy ran, Anderson knew there was something wrong. "What'd he say?" he asked Neil. Though the old man would not admit it, his hearing was beginning to go.

"He says Studs got out into the cows. Sounds like a lotta hooey to me."

"Pray God it is," Anderson replied, and his look fell on Neil like an iron weight.

Anderson ordered Neil back to the village to see that the men did not forget to bring ropes and prods in their hurry to give pursuit. Then with Buddy he set off on the clear trail the herd had made. They were about ten minutes behind them, by Buddy's estimate.

"Too long," Anderson said, and they began to run instead of trotting.

It was easy, running among the Plants, for they grew far apart and their cover was so thick that no underbrush could grow. Even fungi languished here, for lack of food. The few aspens that still stood were rotten to the core and only waiting for a strong wind to fell them. The firs and spruce had entirely disappeared, digested by the very soil that had once fed them. Years before, the plants had supported hordes of common parasites, and Anderson had hoped mightily that the vines and creepers would destroy their hosts, but the Plants had rallied and it was the parasites who had, for no apparent reason, died.

The giant boles of the Plants rose out of sight, their spires hidden by their own massive foliage; their smooth, living green was unblemished, untouched, and like all living things, unwilling to countenance any life but their own.

There was in these forests a strange, unwholesome solitude, a solitude more profound than adolescence, more unremitting than prison. It seemed, in a way, despite its green, flourishing growth, dead. Perhaps it was because there was no sound. The great leaves overhead were too heavy and too rigid in structure to be stirred by anything but gale winds. Most of the birds had died. The balance of nature had been so thoroughly upset that even animals one would not think threatened had joined the ever-mounting ranks of the extinct. The Plants were alone in these forests, and the feeling of their being set apart, of their belonging to a different order of things was inescapable. It ate at the strongest man's heart.

"What's that smell?" Buddy asked.

"I don't smell anything."

"It smells like something burning."

Anderson felt small stirrings of hope. "A fire? But they wouldn't burn at this time of year. They're too green."

"It's not the Plants. It's something else."

It was the smell of roasting meat, but he wouldn't say so. It would be too cruel, too unreasonable to lose one of the precious cows to a party of marauders.

Their pace slowed from a run to a trot, from a trot to a cautious, stalking glide. "I do smell it now," Anderson whispered. He withdrew from its holster the Colt Python .357 Magnum that was the visible sign of his authority among the citizens of Tassel. Since his elevation to his high office (formally, he was the town's mayor, but in fact he was much more), he had never been known to be without it. The potency of this weapon as a symbol (for the village had a goodly stock of guns and ammunition yet) rested upon the fact that it was only employed for the gravest of purposes: to kill men.

The smell had become very strong; then at a turn in the path they found the twelve carcasses. They had been incinerated to ash, but the outlines were clear enough to indicate which had been Studs. There was also a smaller patch of ash near them on the path.

"How——" Buddy began. But he really meant *what,* or even *who,* something that his father was quicker to understand.

"Jimmie!" the old man screamed, enraged, and he buried his hands in the smaller pile of still-smoking ashes.

Buddy turned his eyes away, for too great sorrow is like drunkenness: it was not fitting that he should see his father then.

There's not even any meat left, he thought, looking at the other carcasses. *Nothing but ashes.*

"My son!" the old man cried. "My son!" He held in his finger a piece of metal that had once been the buckle of a belt. Its edges had been melted by the heat, and the metal's retained heat was burning the old man's fingers. He did not notice. Out of his throat came a noise, deeper than groan, and his hands dug into the ashes once more. He buried his face in them and wept.

After a while, the men of the village arrived. One had brought a shovel to use as a prod. They buried the boy's ashes there, for already the wind was beginning to spread them over the ground. Anderson kept the buckle.

While Anderson was speaking the words over his son's shallow grave, they heard the *moo* of the last cow, Gracie. So as soon as they'd said *amen,* they went running after the surviving cow. Except Anderson, who walked home alone.

Gracie led them a merry old chase.

TWO DESERTION

They had to abandon Tassel, the old Tassel that they still thought of as their proper home, the spring before last. The Plants had flung out their seedlings (though exactly how this was done remained a mystery, for the Plants exhibited not the slightest sign of flowers or fruiting bodies) over the surrounding fields with a profligacy that had finally conquered every human effort. They, the humans, had been extended too far: their town and the farms about it had not been laid out with a siege in view.

For the first three years, they had held their own well enough—or so it had seemed—by spraying the seedlings with poisons that the Government had developed. Each year, for as long as the Government and its laboratories lasted, it was a new poison, for the Plant developed immunities almost as quickly as the poisons were invented. But even then they had sprayed only the fields. In marshes and along the wild lake shore, in forests and along the roads, the seedlings shot up beyond the reach of any enemy but the axe—and there were just too many Plants and too few axes to make that a conceivable enterprise. Wherever the Plants grew, there was not light enough, nor water enough, nor even soil enough for anything else. When the old trees and bushes and grasses were crowded out and died, erosion stripped the land.

Not the farmlands, of course—not yet. But in only three years the Plants were crowding the fields and pastures, and then it was only a matter of time. Of very little time, really: the Plants nibbled, they bit, and, during the summer of their fifth year, they simply overran.

All that was left was this shadowy ruin. Buddy took a certain elegiac pleasure in coming here. There was even a practical side to it: scavenging in the debris he was often able to find old tools and sheet metal, even occasional books. The time for edibles was past, though. The rats and marauders working their way up from Duluth had long ago cleaned out the little that had been left behind after the move to New Tassel. So he gave up looking and went to sit on the steps of the Congregationalist Church, which thanks to his father's continued efforts was one of the last buildings in the town to remain intact.

There had been, he remembered, an oak, a tall archetypal oak, over to the right of the Plant that had broken through the sidewalk at the edge of what used to be the town park. During the fourth winter, they had used the oak as firewood. And many elms, too. There had certainly been no lack of elms.

He heard, distantly, Gracie's lugubrious plaint as she was pulled back to town at the end of a rope. The chase had been too much for Buddy. His legs had given out. He wondered if the Hereford was now extinct. Perhaps not, for Gracie was pregnant, she was still young, and if she bore a bull calf, there would be hope for her race, though it were but a glimmer. What more could one ask than a glimmer?

He wondered, too, how many enclaves had held out as long as Tassel. For the last two years, captured marauders had been the village's only link with the outside, But the marauders had been growing fewer. It was likely that the cities had come to their end at last.

He was thankful he had not been there to witness it, for even the little corpse of Tassel could make him melancholic. He would not have thought he could have cared so. Before the advent of the Plants, Tassel had been the objectification of everything he despised: smallness, meanness, willful ignorance and a moral code as contemporary as Leviticus. And now he mourned it as though it had been Carthage fallen to the Romans and sown with salt, or Babylon, that great city.

It was not perhaps the corpse of the town that he mourned, but all the other corpses of which it was compounded. Once a thousand and some people had lived here, and all but a paltry two hundred and forty-seven of them were dead. How invariably the worst had survived and the best had died.

Pastern, the Congregationalist minister, and his wife Lorraine. They had been good to Buddy during the years before he'd left for the University, when life had been one long feud with his father who had wanted him to go to the Ag School in Duluth. And Vivian Sokulsky, his fourth-grade teacher. The only older woman in town with a sense of humor or a grain of intelligence. And all the others too, always the best of them.

Now, Jimmie Lee. Rationally you couldn't blame the Plants for Jimmie's death. He had been murdered—though how or by whom, Buddy could not imagine. Or why. Above all, why? Yet death and the Plants were such close kin that one could not feel the breath of one without seeming to see the shadow of the other.

"Hello there, stranger." The voice had a strong musical timbre, like the speaking voice of the contralto in an operetta, but to judge by Buddy's reaction one would have thought it harsh.

"Hello, Greta. Go away."

The voice laughed, a full, husky laugh that would have reached the last rows of any balcony, and Greta herself came forward, as full and husky in the flesh as in her laughter, which now abruptly ceased. She stood herself before Buddy as though she were presenting a grievance before the court. Exhibit A: Greta Anderson, arms akimbo and shoulders thrown back, full hips jutting forward, her bare feet planted in the dirt like roots. She deserved better clothing than the cotton chemise she wore. In richer fabrics and brighter colors and given better support, the type of beauty Greta represented could excel any other; now she seemed just slightly overripe.

"I hardly ever see you any more. You know we're practically next-door neighbors——"

"Except that we don't have doors."

"—yet I don't see you from one week to the next. Sometimes I think you try to avoid me."

"Sometimes I do, but you can see for yourself it doesn't work. Now, why don't you go fix your husband's dinner like a good wife? It's been a bad day all around."

"Neil's in a blue funk. I expect he'll be whipped tonight, and *I'm* not going to be around the house—or should I say the tent?—when he comes home from that. When he went back to town, he fooled with the rope on Studs's pen to try and make it look like it wasn't his fault—that Studs had jumped over the bar. I can just see Studs clearing an eight-foot fence. But it didn't do him any good. Clay and half a dozen others saw him doing it. He'll just get whipped a little harder now."

"That idiot!"

Greta laughed. "You said it, not me."

With a feigned casualness, she sat on the step below his. "You know, Buddy, I come here a lot too. I get so lonely in the new town—it's not really a town at all, it's more like summer camp with the tents and having to carry water from the stream. Oh, it's so boring. *You* know what I mean. You know it better than me. I always wanted to go live in Minneapolis myself, but first there was Daddy, and then. . . . But I don't have to tell *you*."

It had grown quite dark in the ruined village. A summer shower began to fall on the leaves of the Plants, but only a few droplets penetrated their cover. It was like sitting in spray blown in off the lake.

After a considerable silence (during which she had leaned back to rest her elbows on Buddy's step, letting the weight of her thick, sun-whitened hair pull her head back, so that as she talked she gazed up into the faraway leaves of the Plant), Greta let loose another well modulated laugh.

Buddy couldn't help but admire her laugh. It was as though that laughter was a specialty of hers—a note she could reach that other contraltos couldn't.

"Do you remember the time you put the vodka into the punch at Daddy's youth meeting? And we all started doing the twist to those awful old records of his? Oh, that was precious, that was such fun! Nobody but you and me knew *how* to twist. That was an awful thing to do. The vodka, I mean. Daddy never knew what happened."

"Jacqueline Brewster could twist well, as I recall."

"Jacqueline Brewster is a pill."

He laughed, and since it had become so much less customary for him, the laughter was rough-edged and a little shrill. "Jacqueline Brewster's dead," he said.

"That's so. Well, I guess next to the two of us she *was* the best dancer around." After another pause, she began again with a great show of vivacity. "And the time we went to old man Jenkins' house, out on County Road B—do you remember that?"

"Greta, let's not talk about that."

"But it was so *funny,* Buddy! It was the funniest thing in the world. There we were, the two of us, going at it on that squeaky old sofa a mile a minute. I thought it would fall to pieces, and him upstairs so dead to the world he never knew a thing."

Despite himself, Buddy snorted. "Well, he was *deaf.*" He pronounced the word in the country way, with a long *e.*

"Oh, we'll never have times like that again." When she turned to look at Buddy, her eyes gleamed with something more than reminiscence. "You *were* the wild one then. There wasn't anything that stopped you. You were the king of the heap, and wasn't I the queen? Wasn't I, Buddy?" She grabbed one of his hands and squeezed it. Once her fingernails would have cut his skin, but her fingernails were gone and his skin was tougher. He pulled his hand away and stood up.

"Stop it, Greta. It won't get you anywhere."

"I've got a right to *remember*. It *was* that way, and you can't tell me it wasn't. I know it's not that way any more. All I have to do is look around to see that. Where's Jenkins' house now, eh? Have you ever tried to find it? It's gone; it's simply disappeared. And the football field— where is that? Every day a little more of everything is gone. I went into MacCord's the other day, where they used to have the nicest dresses in town, such as they were. There wasn't a thing. Not a button. It seemed like the end of the world, but I don't know—maybe those things aren't so important. It's people that are most important. But all the best people are gone, too."

"Yes," Buddy said, "yes, they are."

"Except a very few. When you were away, I saw it all happen. Some of them, the Douglases and others, left for the cities, but that was only at the very beginning of the panic. They came back, the same as you—those who could. I wanted to go, but after Momma died, Daddy got sick and I had to nurse him. He read the Bible all the time. And prayed. He made me get down on my knees beside his bed and pray with him. But his voice wasn't so good then, so usually I'd end up praying by myself. I thought it would have looked funny to somebody else—as though it was Daddy I was praying to and not God. But there wasn't anybody left by that time who could laugh. The laughter had just dried up, like Split Rock River.

"The radio station had stopped, except for the news twice a day, and who wanted to hear the news? There were all those National Guard people trying to make us do what the Government said. Delano Paulsen got killed the night they got rid of the National Guard, and I didn't know about it for a week. Nobody wanted to tell me, because after you left, Delano and I went steady. I guess maybe you never knew that. As soon as Daddy got on his feet, he was going to marry the two of us. Really—he really was.

"The Plants seemed to be everywhere then. They broke up the roads and water mains. The old lake shore was just a marsh, and the Plants were already growing there. Everything was so terribly ugly. It's nice now, in comparison.

"But the worst part was the boredom. Nobody had time to have fun. You were gone and Delano was dead and Daddy—well, you can imagine. I shouldn't admit this, but when he died, I was sort of glad.

"Except that was when your father was elected mayor and really started organizing everybody, telling them what to do and where to live, and I thought: 'There won't be room for me.' I was thinking of Noah's ark, because Daddy used to read that one over and over again. I thought: 'They'll take off without *me*.' I was scared. I suppose everybody was scared. The city must have been scary, too, with all those people dying. I heard about that. But I was really *scared*! How do you explain that?

"And then your brother started coming to visit me. He was about twenty-one then and not really bad-looking from a girl's point of view. Except for his chin. But I thought: 'Greta, you've got a chance to marry Japheth.'"

"Who?"

"Japheth. He was one of Noah's sons. Poor Neil! I mean, he really didn't stand a chance, did he?"

"I think you've reminisced enough now."

"I mean, he didn't know anything about girls. He wasn't like you. He was twenty-one, just three months younger than you, and I don't think he even *thought* about girls. He said later it was your father who recommended me! Can you imagine that! Like he was breeding a bull!"

Buddy started walking away from her.

"What should I have done? You tell me. Should I have waited for you? Put a candle burning in the window?"

"You don't need a candle, when you're carrying a torch."

Again the lyric laugh, but barbed with undissimulated shrillness. She rose and walked toward him. Her breasts, which had been noticeably slack before, were perceptibly less so.

"Well, do you want to know why? You don't. You're afraid to hear the truth. If I told you, you wouldn't let yourself believe it, but I'll tell you anyway. Your brother is a two-hundred pound noodle of wet spaghetti. He is completely and totally unable to *move.*"

"He's my *half*-brother," Buddy said, almost automatically.

"And he's half of a husband for me." Greta was smiling strangely, and somehow they had come to be standing face to face, inches apart. She had only to stand on tiptoe for her lips to reach his. Her hands never even touched him.

"No," he said, pushing her away. "It's over. It's been over for years. That was eight years ago. We were kids then. Teenagers."

"Oh brother, have you lost your guts!"

He slapped her hard enough to knock her to the ground, though in fairness it must be said that she seemed to cooperate and even to relish the blow.

"That," she said, the old music quite gone for her voice, "is all the best that Neil can do. And I must say that between the two of you he does that better."

Buddy laughed a solid, good-humored laugh and left her, feeling some of the old stallion blood rising in him. Ah, he had forgotten what a magnificent wit she could muster. Absolutely the only one left with a sense of humor, he thought. And still the best-looking. Maybe they *would* get together again.

Eventually.

Then he remembered that it was not a day to be in a good humor, and the smile left his lips and the stallion quieted and went back to his stall.

THREE **A BUNDLE OF JOY**

There was something of the mouse about Maryann Anderson. *Mouse* was the color of her hair: a lusterless gray-brown. There was a mousy tendency, when her mind was on other things, for her lips to part, revealing largish, yellowed incisors. Worse, she had, at the age of twenty-three, a faint, downy mustache. She was short, no more than five feet two, and thin: Buddy's thumb and middle finger could completely encircle her upper arm.

Even her good qualities were mousy: She was perky, industrious and content with scraps. Though she would never be a beauty, she might once have been thought cute. She was submissive. She did not intrude.

Buddy didn't love her. There were times when her very passivity infuriated him. He had been used, on the whole, to something more. Still, it was as hard to find fault with Maryann as it was to find anything particularly to admire. Buddy was comfortably sure that she would never be unfaithful, and as long as his wants were looked after, he didn't really resent Maryann for being his wife.

Maryann, for her part, could not reciprocate this indifference. She was slavishly devoted to her husband and hopelessly, girlishly in love with him. Buddy had always been able to elicit a species of self-sacrificing devotion, though he had usually called for a different sort of sacrifice, and his altars, so to speak, were dark with the blood of his victims. But he had never tried to exert this influence on Maryann, who had only interested him for one brief moment and then not amorously but by her pitiableness.

It had been during the fall of the fourth year after the Plants had come, and Buddy had only just returned to Tassel. A party of marauders, Maryann among them, had somehow worked their way up from Minneapolis. Instead of raiding, they'd been foolish enough to come to the village and *ask* for food. It was unheard of. The invariable rule was for marauders to be executed (hunger could turn the lambs to wolves), but a small controversy arose in this case, because of the seeming good-will of the prisoners. Buddy had been among those in favor of releasing them, but his father—and the majority of the men—insisted on execution.

"Then at least spare the women," Buddy had pleaded, being still rather sentimental.

"The only woman that goes free is the one you take to wife," Anderson had proclaimed, extemporizing the law, as was his way. And quite unexpectedly and out of pure cussedness Buddy had gone and chosen one of them, not even the best-looking one, and made her his wife. The other twenty-three marauders were executed, and the bodies were properly disposed of.

Maryann didn't speak unless spoken to, but in their three years together Buddy had picked up enough bits and pieces of her background to convince himself that her depths were no more interesting than her surfaces.

Her father had been a bank clerk, scarcely more than a teller, and she had worked for one month in a stenographic pool before the world had entirely collapsed. Though she had gone to a parochial grade school and later to St. Bridget's, where she took the commercial course, her Catholicism had never been more than lukewarm at best, with hot flashes around the holidays. In Tassel she was able to adopt Anderson's homemade and apocalyptic brand of Congregationalism without a qualm.

But Maryann's special distinction was not her conversion from papistry: it was the new skill she had brought to Tassel. Once, almost by chance, she had taken a night course in basket-weaving at the CYO. Something in Maryann, something quite fundamental, had responded to the simplicities of that ancient craft. She experimented with the thicker rushes and with swamp grasses, and when the shortages began, Maryann went out on her own and began stripping the smooth green boles of the Plants and shredding their great leaves into raffia. Right to the end, to that day when the Government trucks failed to show up in the city for the morning dole, she went on making her baskets and bonnets and sandals and welcome mats. People thought it silly, and Maryann herself considered it a weakness. That it was the one thing that the poor mouse had ever done well or found more than passing satisfaction in escaped their attention and hers.

In Tassel, Maryann's light was no longer hidden, as it were, beneath a bushel. Her basketry quite transformed the village's way of life. After the fatal summer when the Plants invaded the fields, the villagers (the five hundred who were left) had picked up as many pieces as they could carry and took themselves to the shore of Lake Superior, a few miles away down Gooseberry River. The lake had been receding at a prodigious rate, and in several areas the water was two or three miles from the old, rock-strewn shore line. Wherever the water retreated, the thirsty seedlings sprang up, sank roots, and the process accelerated.

That fall and through the winter, the survivors (their number, like the lake, was always shrinking) worked at clearing as large an area as they could hope realistically to maintain for their own fields the next year. Then they began to sink their own roots. There was little timber but what they could scavenge from the old town. The wood of the Plant was less substantial than balsam, and most of the trees native to the area had already rotted. The villagers had the clay but not the skill to make brick, and quarrying was out of the question. So they spent the winter in a great grass hut, whose walls and roof were woven under Maryann's supervision. It had been a cold, miserable November, but a person could keep his fingers warm weaving. There was a week in December when the panels of the commonroom were blown halfway back to the old village. But by January they had learned to make a weave that was proof against the worst blizzard, and by February the commonroom was downright cozy. It even had a welcome mat at each of the doors.

No one had ever regretted admitting the clever mouse to the village. Except, occasionally, the mouse's husband.

"Why isn't there any dinner?" he asked.

"I was all day with Lady. She's awful upset about Jimmie Lee. Jimmie was her favorite, you know. Your father didn't help much either. He talked all the time about the Resurrection of the Body. He must know by now she doesn't believe the same as he does."

"A person has to eat just the same."

"I'm fixing it, Buddy. As fast as I can. Buddy, there's something——"

"Father's feeling better then?"

"—I wanted to tell you. I never know how your father is feeling. He's acting the same as ever. He never loses control. Neil's going to be whipped tonight—I suppose you heard about that?"

"Serves him right. If he'd fixed the gate shut, that whole thing wouldn't have happened."

"What whole thing, Buddy? How can a person be burnt to ashes like that in the middle of the forest? How can that be?"

"You've got me. It doesn't seem possible. And those cows and Studs, besides. Seven tons of beef turned to ash in less than ten minutes."

"Was it lightning?"

"Not unless it was the lightning of the Good Lord. I suspect it's marauders. They've invented some new kind of weapon."

"But why would they want to kill *cows*? They'd want to steal cows—and kill people."

"Maryann, *I* don't know what happened. Don't ask any more questions."

"There was something I wanted to tell you."

"Maryann!"

Glumly, she went back to stirring the suppawn in the earthenware pot that nestled in the hot embers; to the side, wrapped in cornhusks, were three sunfish that Jimmie Lee had caught that morning at the lake shore.

From now on, with neither milk nor butter to add to the corn meal, they'd have to settle for mush, with an occasional egg whipped in it. One of the nice things about being married to an Anderson had always been the extra food. The meat especially. Maryann hadn't questioned too closely where it all came from; she just took what Lady, Anderson's wife, offered her.

Well, she thought, *there are still hogs and chickens and a lake full of fish. The world hasn't come to an end.* Maybe the hunters could bring in enough after the harvest to make up for the Herefords. A couple of years ago, the hunting had been so good that there'd been talk of turning nomad and following the game, like the Indians used to. Then the deer started falling off. There was a winter of wolves and bears, and then it was just like old times. Except for the rabbits. Rabbits could eat the bark off the Plants. Rabbits were cute, the way they wiggled their noses. She smiled, thinking about the rabbits. "Buddy," she said, "there's something I should talk to you about."

Maryann was talking about something, which was almost an event in itself, but Buddy's mind, after a day like this, didn't seem to focus on things very well. He was thinking of Greta again: the curve of her neck when she'd thrown her head back out on the church steps. The slight protuberance of her Adam's apple. And her lips. Somehow she still had lipstick. Had she worn it just for him?

"What'd you say?" he asked Maryann.

"Nothing. Oh, just nothing."

Buddy had always thought that Maryann would have made the ideal wife for Neil. She had the same chin, and same lack of humor, the same stolid industriousness. They both had front teeth like a rabbit's or a rat's. Neil, who was abject before Greta, would not have found fault with Maryann's passivity. With Maryann in bed, Buddy was always reminded of tenth-grade gym class, when Mr. Olsen had had them do fifty pushups every day. But apparently that aspect of things didn't mean so much to Neil.

It had been a shock to come back and find Greta Pastern married to his half-brother. Somehow he'd been counting on finding her waiting for him. She'd been so large a part of the Tassel he'd left behind.

It had been a touchy situation all around, those first weeks. Buddy and Greta had been anything but secretive during Buddy's last year in Tassel. Their carryings-on were discussed in every bar and over every back fence in town. Greta, the pastor's only child, and Buddy, the eldest son of the richest—and most righteous—farmer in the township, in all Lake County. So it was common knowledge that Greta was a hand-me-down in the Anderson family, and a common expectation that something bad would come of it.

But the prodigal who had returned to Tassel was not the same as the prodigal who had left. In the meantime he had starved a third of his weight away, worked on the Government's pressed-labor crews, and butchered his way to Tassel from Minneapolis, joining the human wolf packs or fighting them as the occasion offered. By the time he got to Tassel, he was much more interested in saving his own hide than in getting under Greta's skirts.

So, besides being a humanitarian gesture, it had been prudent to marry Maryann. Buddy as a husband seemed much less likely to breach the village peace than Buddy as a bachelor, and he could pass Greta on the street without causing a storm of speculation.

"Buddy?"

"Tell it to me later!"

"The suppawn's ready. That's all."

Such a ninny, he thought. But a passable cook. Better, leastways, than Greta, and that was a consolation.

He shoveled the steaming, yellow porridge into his mouth, nodding to Maryann that he was satisfied. She watched him put down two bowls of the suppawn and the three fish, then she ate what was left.

I'll tell him now, while he's in a good mood, she thought. But before she could get a word in, Buddy was up off the mat on the floor of the tent and heading outside.

"It must be about time for the whipping," he said.

"I don't want to see it. It makes me sick."

"Nothing says a woman has to go." And with half a smile to cheer her up, he was out of the tent. Even if he had been squeamish (which he wasn't), he would have had to be there, as did every male in the village over seven years old. A good whipping could instill almost as much fear of the Lord in the hearts of beholders as in the single heart about which the lash curled.

In the square before the commonhouse, Neil was already strung up to the whipping post. His back was bare. Buddy was one of the last to arrive.

Anderson, with the whip in his hand, stood spraddle-legged in readiness. There was just a bit too much stiffness in his stance. Buddy knew that it must be costing the old man to carry on as though this were no more than an ordinary fiasco, a matter of some twenty lashes.

When Anderson had to whip Buddy or Neil, he meted out the pain impartially—no more and no less than he would have doled out to anyone else for the same offense. His touch was as precise as a metronome. But tonight, after the third stroke, his knees collapsed and he fell to the ground.

There was a gasp from the circle of spectators, then Anderson was on his feet again. The color had run out of his face, and, giving the whip to Buddy, his hand trembled.

"You continue," he commanded.

If the old man had handed him his Python—or a scepter—Buddy couldn't have been any more taken aback.

Maryann heard it all from inside the tent, while she licked the pot. When there was a pause after the third strike, she hoped that might be the end. She understood of course that these things had to be done, but that didn't mean she had to like it. It wasn't good manners to enjoy someone else being hurt, even if you didn't like them.

The whipping started again.

She wished Buddy had left her more food. And now, with the Guernseys all dead, there'd be no more milk!

She tried to think of what she would say when he got home. She decided on "Darling, we are going to have a bundle of joy."

It was such a nice expression. She had heard it first in a movie a long time ago. Eddie Fisher and Debbie Reynolds had been the stars.

For *his* sake, she hoped it was a boy, and she fell asleep wondering what his name should be. Patrick, for his grandfather? Or Lawrence? She had always loved that name, for some reason. Joseph was a good name too.

Buddy? She wondered if there was a Saint Buddy. She had never heard of one. Perhaps he was a Congregationalist saint.

FOUR GOOD-BYE, WESTERN CIVILIZATION

*O**n** 22 August 1979, as per instructions of 4 July 1979, preparations were begun for the incineration of the artifact shown in the maps as "Duluth-Superior." Meteorological conditions were ideal: for 17 days there had been no rain, scarcely a dampness in the mornings. "Duluth-Superior" was quartered, and each of these Quarters was divided into three Sections, as shown in the accompanying photographs, taken from elevation 1.33 kms. Action began at 20.34 hours, 23 August 1979.*

This artifact was constructed upon numerous low mounds of natural formation, topographically akin to the artifact "San Francisco." Here, however, the major construction element was wood, which burns quickly. Firing began in the lowest areas of each Section, and the natural updraft of air accomplished almost as much as the firing devices.

With the exceptions of Sections II-3 and III-1 near the old lakeshore (here for some reason, the elements of the artifact were larger and constructed of stone and brick instead of wood), complete incineration was achieved in 3.64 hours. When the work in each Quarter had been accomplished to satisfaction, the equipment of that Quarter was transferred to Sections II-3 and III-1, and these Sections were incinerated by 01.12 hours, 24 August 1979.

There were two mechanical failures in Section IV-3. Appraisal of damages has been sent to the Office of Supplies, and a carbon of that appraisal is enclosed herewith.

Mammals dwelling in the periphery of Quarters I, II, and IV escaped into the adjacent fields due to the insufficiency of equipment and the openness of the terrain. Current estimates are from 200 to 340 of the large mammals, constructors of the artifacts, and from 15,000 to 24,000 of the small mammals, within established limits of probable error.

All wood-burrowing insects were eradicated.

Operations have been begun to trace the escaped mammals and other mammals living beyond the limits of "Duluth-Superior," but equipment is limited. (Consult Requisition Form 800-B: 15 August 1979; 15 May 1979; 15 February 1979.)

Following incineration, ash was leveled into the concavities of the artifact, and seeding operations were begun 27 August 1979.

Based on the results of samples taken from 12 May 1979 to 4 July 1979, this unit then removed to follow a route along the southern shore of "Lake Superior." (Consult map of "Wisconsin State.") Sampling had indicated that this area was most densely populated with indigenous mammals.

The obsolete Spheroid Model 37-Mg will be employed for this operation, due to the shortages of Models 39-Mg and 45-Mh. Despite their bulkiness, these models are adequate for the extermination of such mammalian life as they are likely to encounter. Indeed, their thermotropic mechanisms are more highly developed than those of the later models. However, in exceptional circumstances the operation of Model 37-Mg cannot, without undue delay, be assumed by the Central Intelligence Bank of this Unit.

The further process of incineration is expected to proceed less rapidly now that this, the last of the chief artifacts, has been leveled and sown. The remaining artifacts are small and widely spaced. Though our sample has shown that most of these are no longer inhabited, we will, pursuant to instructions of 4 July 1979, effect their entire incineration.

Estimated completion of project: 2 February 1980.

"What do you make of it, my dear?" he asked.

"It's very beautiful," she said. "And did you do it just for me?"

"Sweetheart, as far as I'm concerned, you're the only girl in the world."

Jackie smiled, her bittersweet smile, the one she reserved for hopeless disasters. She closed her eyes, not to shut out the scene, but because they were very tired, and shook the ash from her short, curling black hair.

Jeremiah Orville closed her in his arms. It wasn't chilly, but it seemed the right thing to do just then—a traditional gesture, like taking off one's hat at a funeral. Calmly, he watched the city burn.

Jackie was rubbing her bobbed nose in the scratchy wool of his sweater. "I never really liked that city anyhow," she said.

"It kept us alive."

"Of course, Jerry. I didn't mean to be ungrateful. I just meant——"

"I understand. That's just my well known sentimentality getting out of hand again."

Despite the heat and his enclosing arms, she shivered. "We'll die now. We'll die for sure."

"Chin up, Miss Whythe! Tally-ho! Remember the Titanic!"

She laughed. "I feel like Carmen, in the opera, when she turns up the Queen of Spades." She hummed the Fate theme, and when the last note proved too low, she mumbled: "In an amateur production."

"It's no wonder one feels depressed, with the world burning up about one," he said in his best David Niven manner. Then, in an authentic Midwestern accent: "Hey, look! There goes the Alworth Building!"

She turned around quickly, and her dark eyes danced in the light of the pyre. The Alworth Building was the tallest in Duluth. It burned magnificently. The whole downtown area was in flames now. To the left of the Alworth Building, the First American National Bank, after a late start, flared up even more splendidly due to its greater bulk.

"Ooowh," Jackie shouted. "Wheee!"

They had lived these last three years in the safe-deposit vault in the basement of the First American National Bank. Their precious store of scavenged cans and jars was still locked in the safe deposit boxes, and the canary was probably in his cage in the corner. It had been a very cozy home, though there were few visitors and they had had to kill most of those. Such luck couldn't last forever.

Jackie was crying real tears.

"Sad?" he asked.

"Oh, not sad . . . just a little déracinée. And annoyed with myself, because I don't understand it." She snuffled loudly, and the tears were all gone. "It's so horribly like what they used to call an Act of God. As though God were the source of everything unreasonable. I like to know the reason for things." Then, after a pause: "Perhaps it was the termites?"

"The termites!" He looked at her unbelievingly, and her cheek began to show its tell-tale dimple. She was pulling his leg. They broke out laughing together.

In the distance, the Alworth Building collapsed. Beyond, in the dry harbor, a ship lay on its side and squirted flames out of its portholes.

Here and there, scuttling about the rubble, the incendiary mechanisms could be glimpsed attending their business. At this remove they seemed really quite innocuous. They reminded Jackie of nothing so much as of Volkswagens of the early Fifties, when all Volkswagens seemed to be gray. They were diligent, tidy, and quick.

"We should be getting on our way," he said. "They'll be mopping up the suburbs soon."

"Well, good-bye, Western Civilization," Jackie said, waving at the bright inferno, unafraid. For how can one be afraid of Volkswagens?

They coasted their bicycles along the Skyline Parkway from which they had viewed the burning city. When the Parkway went up hill, they had to walk the bicycles, because the chain on Orville's was broken.

The Parkway, unmended for years, was full of potholes and cluttered with debris. Coming down from Amity Park, they were in the dark, for the hill cut off the light of the fire. They went slowly with their hand-brakes on.

At the bottom of the hill, a clear womanly voice addressed them out of the darkness: *Stop!* They jumped off the bicycles and spread themselves flat on the ground. They had practiced this many times. Orville pulled out his pistol.

The woman stepped into view, her arms over her head, hands empty. She was quite old—that is to say, sixty or more—and defiantly innocent in manner. She came much too close.

"She's a decoy," Jackie whispered.

That much was obvious, but where the others were Orville could not tell. Trees, houses, hedges, stalled cars stood all about. Each would have been an adequate cover. It was dark. The air was smoky. He had lost, for the while, his night vision by watching the fire. Determining to make a show of equal innocence, he reholstered his gun and stood up.

He offered his hand to the woman to shake. She smiled, but did not approach that near.

"I wouldn't go over that next rise, my dears. There's some kind of machine on the other side. Some sort of flame-thrower, I think. If you like, I'll show you a better way to go."

"What does it look like, this machine?"

"None of us have seen it. We've just seen the people who got crisped when they got to the top of the hill. Shocking."

It was not impossible nor even unlikely; it was equally possible and likely that he was being led into a trap. "One moment," he told the woman. He signaled to Jackie to stay where she was and walked up the gentle slope of the hill. He scanned the debris that the years had heaped there and selected a strip of lathing that must have dropped from a load of firewood. Halfway up the hill he stopped behind one of the Plants that had broken through the asphalt. He hurled the stick of lathing over the crest of the hill.

Before it reached the top of its arc it flared into flame, and before it fell out of sight, the flame was dead. The wood had been utterly consumed.

"You're right," he said, returning to the woman. "And we thank you."

Jackie rose to her feet. "We don't have any food," she announced, less to the old woman than to those she supposed were surrounding them. The habit of distrust was too strong to break in an instant.

"Don't worry, my dears, you've passed your first test, such as it is. As far as we're concerned, you've shown your mettle. If you only knew how many people walk right on up. . . ." She sighed. "My name's Alice Nemerov, R.N. Call me Alice." Then, almost as an afterthought: "The letters mean I'm a nurse, you know. If you get sick, I can tell you the name of what you've got. Even help a little, sometimes."

"My name's Jeremiah Orville, M.S. Call me Orville. My letters mean I'm a mining engineer. If you have any mines, I'll be happy to look at them."

"And you, my dear?"

"Jackie Janice Whythe. No letters. I'm an actress, for the love of God! I have thin hands, so I used to do a lot of soap commercials. But I can shoot, and I don't have any scruples that I know of."

"Splendid! Now come along and meet the other wolves. There are enough of us to make a tidy pack. Johnny! Ned! Christie! All of you!" Shards of shadows disengaged themselves from the static darkness and came forward.

Jackie hugged Orville about the waist delightedly. She pulled at his ear, and he bent down for her to whisper in it. "We're going to survive after all! Isn't that wonderful?"

It was more than they had expected.

All his life he had hoped, had Jeremiah Orville, for better things. He had hoped when he started college to become a research scientist. Instead he had drifted into a comfortable job with more security (it had seemed) than San Quentin. He had hoped to leave his job and Duluth as soon as he had saved $10,000, but before the fabled sum, or even half of it, was put together, he was married and the owner of a nice suburban home ($3,000 down, ten years to pay the balance). He had hoped for a happy marriage, but by then (he married late, at age 30) he had learned not to hope too hard. By 1972, when the Plants came, he was at the point of transferring all these choice hopes to the slender shoulders of his four-year-old son. But little Nolan proved unable to support even the burden of his own existence during the first famine that hit the cities, and Therese lasted only a month or two longer. He heard of her death by chance the following year: shortly before she had died he had deserted her.

Like everyone else, Orville pretended to hate the invasion (in the cities it was never considered anything but that), but secretly he relished it, he gloried in it, he wanted nothing else. Before the invasion, Orville had been standing on the threshold of a gray, paunchy middle age, and suddenly a new life—life itself!—had been thrust upon him. He (and anyone else who survived) learned to be as unscrupulous as the heroes in the pulp adventure magazines he'd read as a boy—sometimes, as unscrupulous as the villains.

The world might die about him. No matter: *he* was alive again.

There had been the intoxication, while it lasted, of power. Not the cool, gloved power of wealth that had ruled before, but a newer (or an older) kind of power that came from having the strength to perpetuate extreme inequity. Put more bluntly, he had worked for the Government. First, as a foreman over pressed-labor gangs; later (within only a few months, for the pace of events was speeding up), as the director of the city's entire labor operation. At times, he wondered what difference there was between himself and, say, an Eichmann, but he didn't let his speculations interfere with his work.

In fact it was this, the strength of his imagination, that let him see the untenability of the Government's position and make suitable preparations for its collapse. The farmers could not be driven much further. They had the habit of independence and resented the parasitism of the cities. They would revolt and keep their little food to themselves. Without rations, the slaves in the city (for, of course, that's what they were— slaves) would either revolt or die. In any case, they would die. So (after suitable bureaucratic fictions and a few bribes had had the building condemned), Orville had provisioned his fortress in the basement of the First American National Bank and retired from his life of public service.

There had even been a romance, and it had progressed (unlike his marriage) exactly as a romance should progress: a strongly contested courtship, extravagant declarations, fevers, jealousies, triumphs—oh unceasing triumphs, and always the aphrodisiac of mortal danger that suffused the alleys and looted stores of the dying city.

Three years he had been with Jackie Whythe, and it seemed no more than a holiday weekend.

If it were true for him, would it not be true for the other survivors as well? Did they not all feel this clandestine gladness in their hearts, like adulterers together secretly in a strange town? It must be so, he thought. It must be so.

Past the Brighton Beach Tourist Camp, the Plants grew denser and the urban sprawl thinned. The fortuitously met little group had come to the wilderness, where they might be safe. As they moved northeast on Route 61, the dim light of the burning city faded behind them, and the dimmer light of the stars was blotted out by foliage. They advanced into perfect darkness.

They moved rapidly, however, for though the Plants had broken through the road wherever they wished, they had not obliterated it. It was not as though the hurrying band had to fight its way through one of the old scrub woods that had once grown around here: no branches tore at one's face; no brambles snagged one's feet. There were not even mosquitoes, for the Plants had drained all the marshes roundabout. The only obstructions were occasional potholes, and sometimes, where the Plants had broken the asphalt sufficiently to give headway to erosion, a gulley.

Orville and the others followed the highway until morning glowed grayly through the eastern mass of forest, then turned toward the light, toward the lake, which had once been visible to the cars driving along this road. It seemed dangerous to follow Route 61 any farther, as though it were an extension of the city and subject to the city's fate. Then, too, they were thirsty. If luck was with them, they might even get fish from the lake.

The route had been forced on them by circumstances. It would have been wiser, with the winter in view, to move south, but that would have meant circling the burning city, a chance in no way worth taking. There was no water to the west, and to the east there was too much. Lake Superior, though diminished, was still an effective barrier. Perhaps one of the lake-shore villages would have maintained serviceable boats, in which case they might turn pirate, as that fleet of tugboats had done three years before when Duluth Harbor ran dry. But the best probable direction was to continue northeast along the shore of the lake, looting the farms and villages. Worry about winter when winter came.

Lake Superior teemed with sunfish. Cooked over a driftwood fire, they were good even without salt. Afterward the group discussed, with some attempt at optimism, their plight and prospects. There was not much to decide: the situation dictated its own terms. The gathering was in fact less a discussion than a contest among the sixteen men to see who would assume leadership. Their band had been formed at hazard. Except for the couples, they did not know each other. (There had been little social life those last years; the only community that had survived in the cities had been the pack, and if any of these men had been in a pack before, he wasn't talking about it now.) None of the contenders for leadership seemed willing to discuss the details of his own survival.

Such reticence was natural and becoming: at least they had not become so brutalized as to exult in their depravity and brag of their guilt. They had done what they had to, but they were not necessarily proud of it.

Alice Nemerov rescued them from this awkwardness by narrating her own story, which was singularly free of unpleasantnesses, considering. From the very first days of the famine she had stayed at the main hospital, living in the isolation ward. The hospital personnel had traded on its skills and medical supplies and gotten through even the worst times—except, apparently, for that last worst time of all. The survivors were mostly nurses and interns; the doctors had retired to their country houses when, after the failure of the Government, anarchy and famine had governed the city. In the last years, Alice Nemerov had gone about the city, armored in innocence and the certain knowledge that her skills would be a passport among even the meanest survivors, secure also in the knowledge that she had passed quite beyond the point where she need worry about rape. Thus, she had come to know many of her fellow refugees, and she effected their introductions with aplomb and tact. She told too of other survivors and the curious expedients by which they had saved themselves from starvation.

"Rats?" Jackie asked, trying not to seem overdelicate in her disgust.

"Oh yes, my dear, lots of us tried that. I'll admit it was highly unpleasant." Several of her listeners shook their heads in agreement.

"And there were cannibals, too, but they were poor guilty souls, not at all what you'd think a cannibal would be like. They were always pathetically eager to talk, for all of them lived quite alone. Fortunately, I never came across one when he was hungry, or my feeling might be different."

As the sun mounted to noonday, weariness and sheer contiguity made the others drop their guards and speak of their own pasts. Orville realized for the first time that he was not quite the monster of iniquity that he had sometimes thought himself. Even when he revealed that he had been a foreman on the Government labor crews, his hearers did not seem outraged or hostile, though several of them had been impressed for labor in their time. The invasion had turned everyone into relativists: as tolerant of each other's ways and means, as if they were delegates at a convention of cultural anthropologists.

It was hot, and they needed sleep. The breaking down of the barriers of solitude had tired their spirits almost as much as the march had tired their bodies.

The band did post sentinels, but one of them must have slept. The opportunity for resistance was already past before it was realized.

The farmers—their bones as ill-clothed with flesh as that flesh with tattered denim—outnumbered them three to one, and the farmers had been able, while the wolves slept (lambs, might not one better say?) to confiscate most of the weapons and prevent the use of the rest.

With one exception: Christie, whom Orville had thought he might grow to like, had managed to shoot one farmer, an old man, in the head. Christie was garroted.

Everything happened very quickly, but not too quickly for Jackie to give Orville a last kiss. When she was pulled away from him, roughly, by a younger farmer who seemed better fleshed-out than the majority, she was smiling the special, bittersweet smile which was reserved for just such occasions as this.

FIVE BLOOD RELATIONS

Lady tucked Blossom into bed that night just as though she were still her little girl. She *was* only thirteen after all. Outside the men were still going at it. It was a terrible thing. If only she could shut her ears to it.

"I wish they didn't have to do that, Mother," Blossom whispered.

"It's necessary, darling—a necessary evil. Those people wouldn't have hesitated to kill us. Are you warm under that thin blanket?"

"But why don't we just *bury* them?"

"Your father knows best, Blossom. I'm sure it distresses him to have to do this. I remember that your brother Buddy—" Lady always referred to her stepson as Blossom's and Neil's brother, but she could never forget that this was a half-truth at best and she stumbled over the word. "—that he once felt the same as you."

"*He* wasn't there tonight. I asked Maryann. She said he'd gone out to the west field."

"To guard against the other marauders who may come." The steady rasping noise outside penetrated the light weave of the summer walls and hung in the air. Lady brushed back a strand of gray hair and composed her features to something like sternness. "I have work to do now, darling."

"Would you leave the light?"

Blossom knew better than to burn oil to no purpose—even this oil, which had been extracted from the Plant. She was only seeing how far she could go. "Yes," Lady conceded (for it was not just any night), "but keep it very low."

Before she lowered the curtain that partitioned Blossom's bed from the rest of the commonroom, she asked if Blossom had said her prayers.

"Oh, *Mother*!"

Lady lowered the curtain without either condoning or reproaching her daughter's ambiguous protest. Her husband, certainly, would have seen it as an impiety—and punishable.

Lady could not help being pleased that Blossom was not *so* impressionable (and if the girl had a fault, it was that) as to be led too fervently or too fearfully to adopt her father's fierce, unreasoning Calvinism. If one had to behave like an infidel, Lady believed, it was sheer hypocrisy to pass oneself off as a Christian. Indeed, she very much doubted whether the god to whom her husband prayed existed. If he did, why pray to him? He had made His choice some eons ago. He was like the old Aztec gods who had demanded blood sacrifice on their stone altars. A jealous, vengeful god; a god for primitives; a bloody god. What was the scripture Anderson had chosen last Sunday? One of the minor prophets. Lady shuffled through the pages of her husband's great Bible. There it was, in Nahum: "God is jealous, and the Lord revengeth; the Lord revengeth, and is furious; the Lord will take vengeance on his adversaries, and he reserveth wrath for his enemies." Ah, that was God all over!

When the curtain was down, Blossom crawled out of bed and obediently said her prayers. Gradually the rote formulas gave way to her own requests—first, for impersonal benefactions (that the harvest be good, that the next marauders be luckier and escape), then for more delicate favors (that her hair might grow faster so that she could set it in curls again, that her breasts would fill out just a little more, though they were already quite full for her age—for which she gave thanks). At last, snuggling back in bed, these formal requests gave way to mere wishful thinking, and she longed for the things which were no longer or which were yet to be.

When she fell asleep, the machinery outside was still grinding on.

A noise woke her, something woke her. There was still a little light from the lamp. "What is it?" she asked sleepily.

Her brother Neil was standing at the foot of her bed. His face was strangely vacant. His mouth was open: his chin hung slack. He seemed to see her, but she could not interpret the expression in his eyes.

"What is it?" she asked again, more sharply.

He did not reply. He did not move. He was wearing the pants he had worn all that day and there was blood on them.

"Go away, Neil. What did you want to wake me up for?"

His lips moved, as though in sleep, and his right hand made several gestures, emphasizing the unspoken words of his dream. Blossom pulled her thin cover up to her chin and sat up in bed. She screamed, having only meant to tell him to go away a little louder, so he would hear her.

Lady slept lightly, and Blossom did not have to scream more than once. "Are you having nightmares, my—Neil! What are you doing here? Neil?"

"He won't say anything, Mother. He just stands there and he won't answer me."

Lady grabbed her oldest son—now that Jimmie was dead, her *only* son—by the shoulder and shook him roughly. The right hand made more emphatic gestures, but the eyes seemed to stare less raptly now. "Huh?" he mumbled.

"Neil, you go to Greta now, do you hear? Greta is waiting for you."

"Huh?"

"You've been sleepwalking—or something. Now get along." She had already pulled him away from the bed and let the curtain drop, veiling Blossom. She was a few more minutes seeing Neil out the door, then she returned to the trembling Blossom.

"What did he want? Why did he——"

"He's been upset by the things that happened tonight, darling. Everyone is nervous. Your father went out walking and he isn't back yet. It's only nerves."

"But why did he——"

"Who knows why we do the things we do in our dreams? Now, you'd better get to sleep again. Have your own dreams. And tomorrow——"

"But I don't understand."

"Let's hope Neil doesn't either, love. And tomorrow, not a word of this to your father, do you understand? Your father's been upset lately, and it's best that we keep it a secret. Just the two of us. Do you promise?"

Blossom nodded. Lady tucked her into bed. Then she went back to her own bed and waited for her husband to return. She waited till dawn, and all the while, outside, the sausage machine kept up its dreary rasping song.

Waking was pain. Consciousness was consciousness of pain. Movement was painful. It was painful to breathe.

Eddying in and out of the pain were figures of women—an old woman, a girl, a beautiful woman, and a very old woman. The beautiful woman was Jackie, and since Jackie was dead he knew he was hallucinating. The very old woman was the nurse, Alice Nemerov, R.N. When she came it was more painful, so he knew she must be real. She moved his arms and, worse, his leg. *Stop that,* he thought. Sometimes he would scream. He hated her because she was alive, or because she was causing his pain. He was alive too, it seemed. Otherwise, would he feel this pain? Or was it the pain that kept him alive? Oh, stop it. Sometimes he could sleep. That was best.

Ah, Jackie! Jackie! Jackie!

Soon it was more painful to think than anything else, even than having his leg moved. He was no more able to stop or diminish this pain than those that had preceded it. He lay there, while the three women came and went—the old woman, the girl and the very old woman—thinking.

The girl talked to him.

"Hello," she said, "how are you feeling today? Can you eat this? You can't eat anything if you won't open your mouth. Won't you open your mouth? Just a little? Like that—that's fine. Your name's Orville, isn't it? My name's Blossom. Alice told us all about you. You're a mining engineer. It must be very interesting. I've been in a cave, but I've never seen a mine. Unless you call the iron pits mines. They're just holes, though. Open a little wider, that's better. In fact, that's why Daddy——" She stopped. "I shouldn't talk so much though. When you're better, we can have long talks."

"That's why what?" he asked. It was more painful to talk than to eat.

"That's why Daddy said to . . . said not to . . . I mean, both you and Miss Nemerov are alive, but we had to . . ."

"Kill."

"Yes, we had to, all the rest."

"The women too?"

"But you see, we had to. Daddy explains it better than I do, but if we didn't do that, then the others would come back, a lot of them together, and they're very hungry, and we don't have enough food, even for ourselves. The winter is so cold. You can understand that, can't you?"

He didn't say anything more for some days.

It was as though, all that time, he had lived only for Jackie, and with her gone he no longer had any need to live. He was drained of desire for anything but sleep. When she had been alive, he had not known that she had meant so much to him, that anything could. He had never plumbed the measure of his love. He should have died with her; he had tried to. Only the pain of memory could ease the pain of regret, and nothing could ease the pain of memory.

He wanted to die. He told this to Alice Nemerov, R.N.

"Watch your tongue," she counseled, "or they'll oblige you. They don't trust the two of us. We shouldn't even talk together, or they'll think we're plotting. And you'd better try and get well again. Eat more. They don't like you laying around not working. You understand what saved your life, don't you? I did. You're a damn fool to let them break your leg for you. Why wouldn't you talk? They only wanted to know your occupation?"

"Jackie, was she——"

"It wasn't any different for her than for the rest. You saw the machines. But you've got to get your mind off her. *You*—you're lucky to be alive. Period."

"The girl who feeds me—who is she?"

"Anderson's daughter. He's the one in charge here. The wiry old man with the constipated look. Watch out for him. And his son, the big one, Neil. He's worse."

"I remember him from that night. I remember his eyes."

"But most of the people here aren't any different from you and me. Except they're organized. They're not bad people. They only do what they have to do. Lady, for instance, Blossom's mother, is a fine woman. I have to go now. Eat more."

"Can't you eat more than that?" Blossom scolded. "You have to get your strength back."

He picked up the spoon again.

"That's better." She smiled. There was a deep dimple in her freckled cheek when she smiled. Otherwise, it was a commonplace smile.

"What is this place? Does just your family live here?"

"It's the commonroom. We only have it for the summer, because Daddy's the mayor. Later when it's cold, the whole town moves in. It's awfully big, bigger than you can see from here, but even so it gets crowded. There's two hundred and forty-six of us. Forty-eight, with you and Alice. Tomorrow do you think you can try walking? Buddy, he's my brother, my other brother, made a crutch for you. You'll like Buddy. When you're healthy again, you'll feel better—I mean, you'll be happier. We aren't as bad as you think. We're Congregationalists. What are you?"

"I'm not."

"Then you won't have any trouble about joining. But we don't have a real minister, not since Reverend Pastern died. He was my sister-in-law's father—Greta. You've seen her. She's the beauty among us. Daddy was always important in the church, so when the Reverend died, he just naturally took over. He can preach a good sermon, you'd be surprised. He's actually a very religious man."

"Your father? I'd like to hear one of those sermons."

"I know what you're thinking, Mr. Orville. You think because of what happened to the others that Daddy's bad. But he's not cruel deliberately. He only does what he has to. It was—a necessary evil—what he did. Can't you eat more? Try. I'll tell you a story about Daddy, and then you'll see that you haven't been fair to him. One day last summer, at the end of June, the bull got out and started after the cows. Jimmie Lee—that was his youngest—went out after them. Jimmie Lee was sort of Daddy's Benjamin. He put great stock by Jimmie Lee, though he tried not to show it to us others. When Daddy found Jimmie Lee and the cows, they were all burnt up, just like they say happened in Duluth. There wasn't even a body to carry home, just ashes. Daddy went almost out of his mind with grief. He rubbed the ashes into his face and cried. Then he tried to behave like nothing happened. But later that night he just broke down again, crying and sobbing, and he went off by himself to the grave, where he'd found him, and he just sat there for two whole days. He has very deep feelings, but most of the time he doesn't let them show."

"And Neil? Is he the same way?"

"What do you mean? Neil's my brother."

"He was the one who put the questions to me that night. And to other people that I knew. Is he another one like your father?"

"I wouldn't know about that night. I wasn't there. You've got to rest now. Think about what I told you. And Mr. Orville—try and forget about that night."

There was growing in him a desire and will to survive, but unlike any desire he had known till then, this was a cancerous growth, and the strength it lent his body was the strength of hatred. Passionately, he desired not life but revenge: for Jackie's death, for his own torture, for that whole horrible night.

He had never before felt much sympathy for avengers. The basic premises of blood vengeance had always struck him as rather improbable, like the plot of *Il Trovatore,* so that at first he was surprised to find himself dwelling so exclusively on one theme: Anderson's death, Anderson's agony, Anderson's humiliation.

Initially his imagination was content simply to devise deaths for the old man; then, as his strength grew, these deaths were elaborated with tortures, which finally displaced death entirely. Tortures could be protracted, while death was an end.

But Orville, having himself tasted the bitterest gall, knew that there was a limit beyond which pain cannot be heightened. He desired Anderson to endure the sufferings of Job. He wanted to grind ashes into the man's gray hair, to crush his spirit, to ruin him. Only then would he allow Anderson to know that it had been he, Jeremiah Orville, who had been the agent of his humbling.

So that when Blossom told him the story of how the old man had carried on over Jimmie Lee, he realized what he had to do. Why, it had been staring him in the face!

They had walked all the way to the cornfield together, Blossom and Orville. The leg had mended, but he would probably always have the limp. Now, at least, he could limp on his own—without any other crutch than Blossom.

"And that's the corn that's going to feed us all this winter?" he asked.

"It's more than we really need. A lot of it was meant for the cows."

"I suppose you'd be out there harvesting with the rest of them if it weren't for me." It was the custom, during harvest, for the old women and the younger girls to take over the village duties while the stronger women went out into the fields with the men.

"No, I'm not old enough."

"Oh, come now. You're fifteen, if you're a day."

Blossom giggled. "You're just saying that. I'm thirteen. I won't be fourteen till January 31."

"You could have fooled me. You're very well developed for thirteen."

She blushed. "How old are you?" she asked.

"Thirty-five." It was a lie, but he knew he could get away with it.

Seven years ago, when he had been thirty-five, he had looked older than he did now.

"I'm young enough to be your daughter, Mr. Orville."

"On the other hand, Miss Anderson, you're *almost* old enough to be my wife."

She blushed more violently this time and would have left him except that he needed her for support. This was the farthest he'd walked on his own. They stopped for him to rest.

Except for the harvesting, it was hard to recognize this as September. The Plants did not change color with the seasons: they just folded their leaves like umbrellas to let the snow pass to the ground. Nor was there any hint of autumn spiciness in the air. The cold of the mornings was a characterless cold.

"It's beautiful out here in the country," Orville said.

"Oh yes. I think so too."

"Have you lived here all your life?"

"Yes, here or in the old town." She darted a sideways look at him. "You're feeling better now, aren't you?"

"Yes, it's great to be alive."

"I'm glad. I'm glad you're well again." Impulsively she caught hold of his hand. He answered with a squeeze. She giggled with delight.

They began to run.

This, then, seemed to be the final stage of his years-long reversion to the primitive. Orville could not imagine a more unseemly action than the one he intended, and its baseness only heightened the bloody passion that continued to grow in him. His revenge now demanded more than Anderson, more than the man's entire family. It demanded the whole community. And time to savor their annihilation. He must wring every drop of agony from them, from each of them; he must take them, gradually, to the limit of their capacity for suffering and only then push them over the edge.

Blossom turned in her sleep and her hands clutched at the pillow of corn husks. Her mouth opened and closed, opened and closed, and beads of sweat broke out on her brow and in the dainty hollow between her breasts. There was a weight on her chest, as though someone were pressing her into the earth with his heavy boots. He was going to kiss her. When his mouth opened, she could see the screw turning within. Shreds of ground meat tumbled forth. The screw made a dreary rasping sound.

SIX **THANKSGIVING**

Gray clouds were massing overhead. The ground was dry, bare, gray; no grass, no trees, only the Plants, folded for the winter like parasols, grew here. The dull, autumnal light would thicken at times, and a breeze would pass through the park, picking up the dust. Sitting at the concrete picnic tables on the cold benches, a person could see his own breath. Bare hands grew numb and stiff in the cold. All through the park, people exercised their freezing toes inside their shoes and wished that Anderson would finish saying grace.

Across from the park stood what remained of the Congregationalist Church. Anderson had not let his own people cannibalize the wood from the church, but last winter marauders had stripped off the doors for firewood and broken the windows for fun. The winds had filled the church with snow and dust, and in the spring the oak floor had been covered with a lush green carpet of young Plants. Fortunately it had been discovered in time (for the which they were to be thankful), but even so the floor would probably soon collapse of its own weight.

Buddy, wearing his single surviving suit, shivered as the prayer dragged out its slow length. Anderson, standing at the head of the table, was also wearing a suit for the occasion, but Neil, sitting on his father's left hand and facing Buddy, had never owned a suit. He was bundled in woolen shirts and a denim jacket, enviably snug.

It was the custom of the townspeople, like expatriates who return home on brief visits to establish their legal residence, to celebrate all festive occasions except Christmas here in the old town park. Like so many of the unpleasant and disheartening things they had to do, it was necessary for their morale.

Anderson, having at length established the principle that God Almighty was responsible for their manifold blessings, began to enumerate them. The more salient of these blessings was never directly referred to—that, after seven and a half years, they were all still alive (all of them that were), while so many others, the great majority, were dead. Anderson, however, dwelt on more peripheral blessings, local to that year: the abundance of the harvest, Gracie's continued health in her tenth month with calf (not referring to associated losses), the two recent litters of pigs, and such game as the hunters had come home with. Unfortunately, this had been little (one deer and several rabbits), and a surly, scolding note crept into the prayer. Anderson soon rallied and came to a graceful close, thanking his Creator of the wealth of his great Creation and his Savior for the promise of Salvation.

Orville was the first to respond. His *amen* was reverent and at the same time manly. Neil mumbled something with the rest of them and reached for the jug of whiskey (they called it whiskey), which was still three-quarters full.

Lady and Blossom, who sat together at the end of the table nearest the brick barbecue, began serving the soup. It was faintly reminiscent of rabbit and poorly seasoned with weeds from the lake.

"Dig in!" she said cheerily. "There's plenty more coming."

What else could you say on Thanksgiving?

Since it was an important holiday, the whole family, on both sides, was together. Besides the seven Andersons, there was Mae, Lady's younger sister, and her husband Joel Stromberg, formerly of Stromberg's Lakeside Resort Cabins, and the two little Strombergs, Denny, age ten, and Dora, eight. There were, moreover, the Andersons' special guests (still on probation), Alice Nemerov, R.N., and Jeremiah Orville.

Lady could not help but regret the presence of the Strombergs, for she was certain that Denny and Dora would only remind her husband more forcibly of him who was absent from the table. Then, too, the years had not dealt kindly with her dear sister. Mae had been admired as a beauty in her youth (though probably not to the degree Lady had been), but at forty-five she was a frump and a troublemaker. Admittedly, she still had her flame-red hair, but that only pointed up the decay of what else remained. The only virtue that remained to her was that she was a solicitous mother. Too much so, Lady thought.

Lady had always hated the brassy reverence of the holidays. Now, when there was not even the ritual gluttony of a turkey dinner to alleviate the gloom that underlay the holiday cheer, one's only hope was to be out of it as quickly as possible. She was grateful, at least, to be occupied with the serving. If she were carefully inefficient, she might get out of eating altogether.

"Neil," Greta whispered. "You're drinking too much. You'd better stop."

"Huh?" Neil replied, peering up at his wife (he had the habit, when he ate, of bending down over his food, especially if it was soup).

"You're *drinking* too much."

"I wasn't drinking at all, for gosh sakes!" he said, for the whole table to hear. "I was eating my *soup*!"

Greta cast up her eyes to heaven, a martyr to truth. Buddy smiled at the transparency of her purpose, and she caught his smile. There was a flicker of eyelashes, no more.

"'N any case, it ain't any business of yours *how* much I drink or don't drink. I'll drink just as much as I want." To demonstrate this, he poured himself some more of the liquor distilled from the pulpy leaves of the Plant.

It didn't taste like Jim Beam, but Orville had testified to its purity from his own experience of it in Duluth. It was the first use, as food, that Anderson had been able to find for the Plants, and since he was by no means a teetotaler himself, he'd given the project his blessing. Anderson wanted to frown at the way Neil was swilling it down, but he said nothing, not wanting it to look as though he were taking Greta's side. Anderson was a firm believer in male supremacy.

"Anyone want more soup?" Blossom asked.

"I do," said Maryann, who was sitting between her husband and Orville. She ate all she could get now, for the baby's sake. For her little Buddy.

"And I do," said Orville, with that special smile of his.

"I do, too," said Denny and Dora, whose parents had told them to eat all they could at the dinner, which Anderson was providing.

"Anybody else?"

Everybody else had returned to the whiskey, which tasted unpleasantly like licorice.

Joel Stromberg was describing the progress of his disease to Alice Nemerov, R.N. "And it doesn't really hurt—that's the funny thing. It's just that whenever I want to use my hands they start to shaking. And now my head's the same way. Something's got to be done."

"But I'm afraid, Mr. Stromberg, that nothing can be. There used to be some drugs, but even they didn't work very well. Six months, and the symptoms would reappear. Fortunately, as you say, it doesn't hurt."

"You're a nurse, aren't you?"

He was going to be one of *those*! Very carefully, she began to explain everything she knew about Parkinson's disease, and a few things she didn't. If only she could involve someone else in the conversation! The only other soul within speaking distance was the greedy Stromberg boy, who was snitching drinks from the glass of that foul liquor (one taste had been enough for Alice) sitting before Lady's empty plate. If only Lady or Blossom would stop serving food and sit down for a minute, she could escape from the intolerable hypochondriac. "Tell me," she said, "when did it all start?"

The fish were all eaten, and Blossom began gathering the bones. The moment everyone had been waiting for—the dreadful moment of the main course—could be put off no longer. While Blossom brought round the bowl of steaming polenta into which were stirred a few shreds of chicken and garden vegetables, Lady herself distributed the sausages. A hush fell over the table.

Each of them had a single sausage. Each sausage was about nine inches long and three-quarter inch in diameter. They had been crisped over the fire and came to the table still sizzling.

There is some pork in them, Alice reassured herself. *I probably won't be able to tell the difference.*

Everyone's attention turned to the head of the table. Anderson lifted his knife and fork. Then, fully aware of the solemnity of the moment, he sliced off a piece of hot sausage, put it in his mouth, and began to chew. After what seemed a full minute, he swallowed it.

There, but for the grace of God . . . , Alice thought.

Blossom had turned quite pale, and under the table Alice reached for her hand to lend her strength, though Alice didn't feel an excess of it just then.

"What's everyone waiting for?" Anderson demanded. "There's food on the table."

Alice's attention drifted toward Orville, who was sitting there with knife and fork in hand, and that strange smile of his. He caught Alice's look—and winked at her. Of all things! Or was it at *her*?

Orville cut off a piece of the sausage and chewed it consideringly. He smiled beamishly, like a man in a toothpaste ad. "Mrs. Anderson," he announced, "you are a *marvelous* cook. How do you do it? I haven't had a Thanksgiving dinner like this since God knows when."

Alice felt Blossom's fingers relax and pull out of hers. *She's feeling better, now that the worst is over,* Alice thought.

But she was wrong. There was a heavy noise, as when a bag of meal is dropped to the ground, and Mae Stromberg screamed. Blossom had fainted.

He, Buddy, would not have allowed it, much less have originated and insisted upon it, but then very probably he, Buddy, would not have been able to bring the village through those seven hellish years. Primitive, pagan, unprecedented as it was, there *was* a rationale for it.

It. They were all afraid to call it by its right name. Even Buddy, in the inviolable privacy of his own counsel, shied away from the word for it.

Necessity might have been some justification. There was ample precedent (the Donner party, the wreck of the *Medusa*), and Buddy would have had to go no further than this for an excuse—if they had been starving.

Beyond necessity, explanations grew elaborate and rather metaphysical. Thus, metaphysically, in this meal the community was united by a complex bond, the chief of whose elements was complicity in murder, but this complicity was achieved by a ritual as solemn and mysterious as the kiss by which Judas betrayed Christ; it was a sacrament. Mere horror was subsumed into tragedy, and the town's Thanksgiving dinner was the crime and the atonement, so to speak, in one blow.

Thus the theory, but Buddy, in his heart, felt nothing but the horror of it, mere horror, and nothing in his stomach but nausea.

He washed down another steadfast mouthful with the licorice-flavored alcohol.

Neil, when he had polished off his second sausage, began to tell a dirty joke. They had all, except for Orville and Alice, heard him tell the same joke last Thanksgiving. Orville was the only one to laugh, which made it worse rather than better.

"Where the hell is the deer?" Neil shouted, as though this followed naturally from the punch line.

"What are you talking about?" his father asked. Anderson, when he drank (and today he was almost keeping up to Neil), brooded. In his youth he had had a reputation as a mean fighter after his eighth or ninth beer.

"The *deer*, for Christ's sake! The deer I shot the other day! Aren't we going to have some venison? What the hell kind of Thanksgiving is this?"

"Now, Neil," Greta chided, "you *know* that has to be salted down for the winter. There'll be little enough meat as it is."

"Well, where are the other deer? Three years ago those woods were swarming with deer."

"I've been wondering about that myself," Orville said, and again he was David Niven or perhaps, a little more somberly, James Mason. "Survival is a matter of ecology. That's how I'd explain it. Ecology is the way the different plants and animals live together. That is to say—who eats whom. The deer—and just about everything else, I'm afraid—are becoming extinct."

There was a silent but perceptible gasp from several persons at the table who had thought as much but never dared say so in Anderson's presence.

"God will provide," Anderson interposed darkly.

"Yes, that must be our hope, for Nature alone will not. Just consider what's happened to the soil. This used to be forest soil, podzol. Look at it——" He scooped up a handful of the gray dust on the ground. "Dust. In a couple years, with no grass or brush to hold it down, every inch of topsoil will be in the lake. Soil is a living thing. It's full of insects, worms—I don't know what all."

"Moles," Neil put in.

"Ah, *moles*!" said Orville, as though that cinched it. "And all those things live on the decaying plants and leaves in the soil—or on each other, the way we do. You've probably noticed that the Plants don't shed their leaves. So, except where we plant crops, the soil is dying. No, it's dead already. And when the soil is dead, plants—*our* plants—will not be able to live in it again. Not the way they used to."

Anderson snorted his contempt for so preposterous a notion.

"But deer don't live underground," Neil objected.

"True—they are herbivores. Herbivores need to eat grass. For a while, I suppose, they must have lived on the young Plants springing up near the lakeshore, or else, like rabbits, they can eat the bark from the older Plants. But either that was an inadequate diet nutritionally, or there wasn't enough to go around, or——"

"Or what?" Anderson demanded.

"Or the wild life is being eliminated the way your cows were last summer, the way Duluth was in August."

"You can't prove it," Neil shouted. "I've seen those piles of ashes in the woods. They don't prove a thing. Not a thing!" He took a long swallow from the jug and stood up, waving his right hand to *show* that it couldn't be proved. He did not estimate the position or inertia of the concrete table very well, so that, coming up against it, he was knocked back to his seat and then drawn by gravity to the ground. He rolled in the gray dirt, groaning. He had hurt himself. He was very drunk. Greta, clucking disapproval, got up from the table to help.

"Leave him lay!" Anderson told her.

"Excuse *me!*" she declaimed, exciting grandly. "Excuse me for living."

"What ashes was he talking about?" Orville asked Anderson.

"I haven't the faintest idea," the old man said. He took a swallow from the jug and washed it around in his mouth. Then he let it trickle down his throat, trying to forget the flavor by concentrating on the sting.

Little Denny Stromberg leaned across the table and asked Alice Nemerov if she was going to eat any more of her sausage. She'd taken only a single bite.

"I think not," Alice replied.

"Can I eat it then?" he asked. His blue-green eyes glowed from the liquor he had been sneaking all through the meal. Otherwise, Alice was sure, his were not the sort of eyes to glow. "Please, huh?"

"Don't mind Denny, Miz Nemerov. He doesn't mean to be *rude.* Do you, sweet?"

"Eat it," Alice said, scraping the cold sausage off onto the boy's plate.

Eat it and be damned! she thought.

Mae had just observed that they had been thirteen at the table. ". . . so if you believe the old superstitions, one of us will die before the year's out," she concluded with a gay little laugh, in which only her husband joined. "Well, I do believe it's getting awfully cold here," she added, raising her eyebrows to show that her words bore more than a single meaning. "Though what can you expect at the end of November?"

Nobody seemed to expect anything.

"Mr. Orville, tell me, are you native to Minnesota? I ask because of your accent. It sounds sort of English, if you know what I mean. Are you an American?"

"Mae—really!" Lady scolded.

"He does talk funny, you know. Denny noticed it too."

"Really?" Orville stared at Mae Stromberg intently, as though to count each frizzled red hair, and with the strangest smile. "That's odd. I was raised all my life in Minneapolis. I suppose it's just the difference between the city and the country."

"And you're a city person at heart, just like our Buddy. I'll bet you wish you were back there right now, eh? I know your kind." She winked lewdly to indicate just what kind that was.

"Mae, for heaven's sake———"

But Denny succeeded where Lady could not in bringing Mrs. Stromberg to a stop. He vomited all over the table. The heavings splashed onto the four women around him—Lady, Blossom, Alice, and his mother—and there was a great commotion as the women tried to escape the danger that was threatening anew on Denny's face. Orville couldn't help himself—he laughed. He was joined, fortunately, by Buddy and little Dora, whose mouth was filled with sausage. Even Anderson made a noise that might charitably have been interpreted as laughter.

Buddy excused himself, and Orville rose only a moment later, with more compliments for the cook and a scarcely perceptible gesture in Blossom's direction, which, however, Blossom perceived. Stromberg took his son off into the woods, but not far enough to prevent the rest of them from hearing the whipping.

Neil was asleep on the ground.

Maryann, Dora, and Anderson were left alone at the table. Maryann had been crying off and on all day. Now, since she too had had something to drink, she started to talk: "Oh, I can remember the time . . ."

"Excuse me," said Anderson, leaving the table, and taking the jug with him.

". . . in the old days," Maryann went on. "And everything was so beautiful then—the turkey and the pumpkin pie—and everybody so happy . . ."

Greta, after quitting the table, had gone roundaboutly to the church. Before vanishing into the dark vestibule, she and Buddy, who had watched her all the while, had exchanged a glance and Buddy had nodded *yes*. When the dinner broke up, he followed her there.

"Hello there, stranger!" Apparently she had settled on this gambit permanently.

"Hello, Greta. You were in high form today."

In the vestibule they were out of the line of sight from the picnic grounds. The floor was reassuringly solid. Greta took the nape of Buddy's neck firmly in her two cold hands and pulled his lips to hers. Their teeth gnashed together, and their tongues renewed an old acquaintance.

When he began to pull her closer, she drew back, laughing softly. Having gained what she wanted, she could afford to tease. Yes, that was the old Greta.

"Wasn't Neil drunk?" she whispered. "Wasn't he just stinko?"

The expression in her eyes was not exactly as he remembered it, and he could not tell, of the body beneath her winter clothes, whether it had changed likewise. It occurred to him to wonder how much *he* had changed, but the desire mounting within him overrode such irrelevancies. Now it was he who kissed her. Slowly, in an embrace, they began to sink to the floor.

"Oh no," she whispered, "don't."

They were on their knees thus, when Anderson entered. He did not say anything for a long time, nor did they rise. A strange, sly look came over Greta's face, and Buddy thought that it had been this, nothing but this, which Greta had hoped for. She had chosen the church for that very reason.

Anderson made a gesture for them to get up, and he allowed Greta to leave, after only spitting in her face.

Was this compassion, that he did not demand the punishment that the law—his own law—exacted of adulterers: that they be stoned? Or was it only parental weakness? Buddy could read nothing in the old man's grimace.

"I came here to pray," he said to his son when they were alone. Then, instead of finishing his sentence, he swung his booted foot hard at him, but too slowly—perhaps it was the liquor—for Buddy twisted aside in time and received the kick safely in his hip.

"Okay, boy, we'll take care of this later," Anderson promised, his voice slurring the words. Then he went into the church to pray.

It seemed that Buddy was no longer to enjoy the position he had inherited last June of being foremost in his father's favor. As he left the church, the first snowflakes of the new season drifted down from the gray sky. Buddy watched them melting on the palm of his hand.

SEVEN ADVENT

Gracie the cow lived right there in the commonroom with everybody else. The chickens, likewise, had a corner to themselves, but the pigs were housed in a sty of their own, outside.

For four days, beginning that Thanksgiving, the snow had drifted down, slowly, ponderously, like snow settling on the miniature town inside a glass paperweight. Then for one week of bright wintry weather the children went sledding down the old lakeshore. After that the snow came down in earnest, driven by gale winds that made Anderson fear for the walls, bolstered though they were by the high drifts. Three or four times a day the men went outside to wind back the "awning" that formed the roof of the commonroom. As the half of the roof heavy with snow was cleared off and rolled up, the other half emerged from its weathertight cocoon to replace it. Aside from this chore and the care of the pigs, the men were idle during a blizzard. The rest of the work—cooking, weaving, looking after the children and the sick—was for women. Later, when the weather cleared, they could hunt again or, with more hope of success, fish through the ice of the lake. There were also plenty of Plants to chop down.

It was hard to get through these idle days. Drink wasn't allowed in the commonroom (there were enough fights as it was), and poker soon lost its appeal when the money in the pot was no more valuable than the money the children played with at their unending games of Monopoly. There were few books to read, except Anderson's calf-bound Bible (the same that once had graced the lectern of the Episcopal Church), for indoor space was at a premium. Even if there had been books, it was doubtful that anyone would have read them. Orville might have—he seemed a bookish sort. Buddy would have. And Lady had always read a lot too.

The conversation, such as it was, never rose above the level of griping. For the most part, the men imitated Anderson, who sat immobile on the edge of his bed, chewing the pulp of the Plant. It is questionable, however, whether they spent this time, like Anderson, in thought directed to useful ends. When spring came, all the ideas, the projects, the innovations came from Anderson and no one else.

Now, it appeared, there *was* someone else capable of thought. He, by contrast, preferred to think aloud. To the old man, sitting there listening to Jeremiah Orville, the ideas that were put forth seemed positively irreligious at times. The way he talked about the Plants, for instance— as though they were only a superior laboratory specimen. As though he admired their conquest. Yet he said many things, in almost the same breath, that made good sense. Even when the weather was the subject of conversation (and more often than not it was), Orville had something to say about that.

"I still maintain," Clay Kestner had said (this was on the first day of the bad blizzard, but Clay had been maintaining the same thing for several years), "that it's not the weather getting colder but *us* getting out in the cold more. It's psychosomatical. There ain't no *reason* for the weather to get colder."

"Damn it, Clay," Joel Stromberg replied, shaking his head reprovingly (though it might have been just palsy), "if this winter ain't colder than the winters in the sixties and fifties I'll eat my hat. It used to be that we'd worry whether we was going to have a white Christmas. And I say it's the way the lake has gone down causes it."

"Poppycock!" Clay insisted, not without justice.

Usually no one would have paid any more attention to Clay and Joel than to the wind whining about the spiky Plants outside, but this time Orville intruded: "You know—there *may* be a reason why it's getting colder. Carbon dioxide."

"What's that got to do with the price of eggs?" Clay quipped.

"Carbon dioxide is what the Plants—any plants—take in to combine with water when they're making their own food. It's also what we—that is, animals—exhale. Since the Plants have come, I suspect that the old balance between the carbon dioxide they take in and the amount we give off has started favoring the Plants. So there's less carbon dioxide in the atmosphere. Now, carbon dioxide is a great absorber of heat. It stores heat from the sun and keeps the air warm. So with less carbon dioxide, there'll be a lot more cold and snow. That's just a theory, of course."

"That's a hell of a theory!"

"I'll agree with you there, Clay, since it's not mine. It's one of the reasons geologists give for the ice ages."

Anderson didn't believe strongly in geology, since so much of it went against the Bible, but if what Orville said about carbon dioxide was true, then the worsening of the winters (and they were worse, no one really doubted it) might well have that for a cause. But true or not, there was something he didn't like in Orville's tone, something more than just the know-it-all attitude of the college grad, which Anderson was used to from Buddy. It was as if these little lectures on the wonders of science (and there had been more than a few) had but a single purpose: to lead them to despair.

But he *did* know more science than anyone else, and Anderson grudgingly respected him for it. If nothing else, he'd stopped Clay and Joel from arguing about the weather, and for that small blessing Anderson could not help but give thanks.

It was not as bad yet as it would become in February and March, but it was very bad: the close quarters, the silly quarrels, the noise, the stench, the abrasion of flesh on flesh and nerve on nerve. It was very bad. It was well nigh intolerable.

Two hundred and fifty people lived in 2,400 square feet, and much of that space was given over to storage. Last winter when there had been almost double the number in the same room, when every day witnessed a new death, every month a new epidemic of the deadly common cold, it had been measurably worse. The more susceptible types—those who couldn't bear up—had run amok, singing and laughing, into the deceiving warmth of the January thaws; these were gone this year. This year the walls were firmly anchored and tightly woven from the start; this year the rationing was not so desperately tight (though there *would* be less meat). Yet for all these improvements, it was still an intolerable way to live and everyone knew it.

The thing that Buddy could not stand, the very worst thing, was the presence of so much flesh. All day it rubbed against him, it displayed itself, it stank in his nostrils. And any of the hundred women in the room, even Blossom, would by the simplest gesture, by the tamest word, trigger his lust. Yet for all the good it did him, he might as well have been watching the bloodless phantasms of a movie. There was simply no place, day or night, in the cramped commonroom for sex. His erotic life was limited to such occasions as he could impose upon Maryann to come with him to visit the freezing outhouse by the pig sty. Maryann, in her seventh month and prone at any time to sniffles, seldom accommodated him.

It did not help that, as long as there was daylight in the room, Buddy could look up from whatever he was doing (or more likely—whatever he wasn't doing) and see, probably no more than twenty feet away, Greta.

More and more, he found himself seeking the refuge of Jeremiah Orville's company. Orville was the sort of person, familiar to Buddy from the university, whom he had always liked much more than they had liked him. Though he never once told a joke in Buddy's hearing, when the man talked—and he talked incessantly—Buddy couldn't keep from laughing. It was like the conversations in books and movies or the way people talked on the old Jack Paar show, people who could take the most commonplace thing and, in the telling, make it funny. Orville never tried to clown; his humor was in the way he looked at things—with a certain, sly irreverence (not so much that someone like Anderson could object), an oblique mockery. You never knew where you stood with him, so that most folks—the authentic grassroots hicks like Neil—were reluctant to get into conversations with him, though they listened gladly. Buddy found himself imitating Orville, using *his* words, pronouncing them *his* way (*gen*-uine instead of genu-*wine*), adopting *his* ideas.

It was a constant source of wonder how much the man *knew*. Buddy, who considered his own education barely sufficient to judge the scope of another person's, considered Orville encyclopedic.

Buddy fell so thoroughly under the older man's influence that it would not be unjust to say he was infatuated. There were times (for instance, such times as Orville would talk too long with Blossom) when Buddy felt something like jealousy.

He would have been surprised to learn that Blossom felt much the same way when Orville spent undue time with him. It was quite evidently a case of infatuation, of conventional puppy-love.

Even Neil had a good word to say for the newcomer, for one day Orville had taken him aside and taught him a whole new store of dirty jokes.

The hunters hunted alone; the fishermen fished together. Neil, a hunter, was grateful for the chance to be alone, but the lack of game that December aggravated him almost as much as the shove and clamor of the commonroom. But, the day the blizzard stopped, he found deer tracks cutting right through the still-uncrusted snow of the west cornfield. He followed them four miles, stumbling over his own snowshoes in his eagerness. The tracks terminated in a concavity of ash and ice. No tracks led away from or approached the area. Neil swore loudly. Then he screamed for a while, not really aware that he was screaming. It left off the pressure.

No use hunting now, he thought, when he began to think again. He decided he would rest for the rest of the day. Rest . . . rest! Ha! He'd have to remember that. With the other hunters and fishermen still out of the commonroom, maybe he'd get a little privacy.

That's what he did—he went home and drank a pot of cruddy licorice-flavored tea (that's what they called it, tea) and he got to feeling drowsy and hardly knew what he was looking at or what he was thinking (he was looking at Blossom and thinking of her) when all of a sudden Gracie started making an uproar like he'd never heard before. Except he had heard it before: Gracie was calving.

The cow was making grunting noises like a pig. She rolled over on her side and squirmed around in the dirt. This was Gracie's first calf, and she wasn't any too big. Trouble was only to be expected. Neil knotted some rope into a noose and got it over her neck but she was thrashing around so that he couldn't get it over her legs so he let that go.

Alice, the nurse, was helping him, but he wished his father was there anyhow. Old Gracie was bellowing like a bull now.

Any cow that goes more than an hour is a sure loss, and even half an hour is bad. Gracie was in pain like that and bellowing for half an hour. She kept squirming backward to try and escape the shooting pains. Neil hauled on the rope to keep her from doing that.

"I can see his head. His head's coming out now," Alice said. She was down on her knees in back of Gracie, trying to spread her wider open.

"If that's all you can see, how do you know it's a he?"

The calf's sex was crucial, and everyone in the commonroom had gathered around to watch the calving. After each bellow of pain, the children shouted their encouragement to Gracie. Then her squirming got worse, while her bellowing quieted. "That's it, that's it!" Alice was calling out, and Neil hauled all the harder against the rope.

"It's a boy!" Alice exclaimed. "Thank God, it *is* a boy!"

Neil laughed at the old woman. "It's a *bull* is what you mean. You city slickers are all alike." He felt good because he hadn't made any mistakes and everything was hunky-dory. So he went over to the barrel and got the top off and dipped himself a drink to celebrate. He asked Alice if she wanted one, but she just looked at him funny-like and said no.

He sat down in the room's single easy chair (Anderson's) and watched the little bull-calf sucking at Gracie's full udder. Gracie hadn't got up. She must have been exhausted by the birthing. Why, if Neil hadn't been around, she probably wouldn't of lived through it probably. The licorice flavor wasn't so bad once you got used to it. All the women were quiet now, and the children too.

Neil looked at the bull-calf and thought how someday it'd be a big horny bull mounting Gracie—his own mother! *Animals,* he thought foggily, *are just like animals.* But that wasn't exactly it.

He had some more to drink.

When Anderson got home he looked like he'd had a bad day (was the afternoon gone already?), but Neil got up from the warm chair and called out happily: "Hey, Dad, it's a bull!"

Anderson came up, and he looked the way Neil remembered him looking Thanksgiving night, all dark and with that ugly smile (but he hadn't said a word, then or later, about Neil drinking too much at dinner), and he hit Neil in the face, he just knocked him right down on the floor.

"You goddam stupid asshole!" Anderson yelled. "You dumb turd! Don't you know that Gracie's dead? You strangled her to death, you son of a bitch!"

Then he kicked Neil. Then he went over and cut Gracie's neck where the rope was still right around it. Most of the cold blood went into the basin Lady was holding, but some of it spilled out in the dirt. The calf was pulling at the dead cow's udder, but there wasn't any more milk. Anderson cut the calf's throat, too.

It wasn't *his* fault, was it? It was Alice's fault. He hated Alice. He hated his father too. He hated all those bastards who thought they were so goddam smart. He hated all of them. He hated all of them.

And he cupped his pain in his two hands and tried not to scream from the pain in his hands and the pain in his head, the pain of hating, but maybe he did scream, who knows?

Shortly before dark the snow began to come down again, a perfectly perpendicular descent through the windless air. The only light in the commonroom came from the single hurricane lamp burning in the kitchen alcove where Lady was scouring the well scoured pots. No one spoke. Who dared say how fine the usual mush of cornmeal and rabbit tasted flavored with the blood of cow and calf. It was quiet enough to hear the chickens fussing and clucking in their roosts in the far corner.

When Anderson went outside to direct the butchering and salting down of the carcasses, neither Neil nor Buddy was invited to participate. Buddy sat by the kitchen door on the dirty welcome mat and pretended to read a freshman biology text in the semidarkness. He had read it through many times before and knew some passages by heart. Neil was sitting by the other door, trying to screw up the courage to go outside and join the butchers.

Of all the townspeople, Buddy was probably the only one who took pleasure in Gracie's death. In the weeks since Thanksgiving, Neil had been winning his way back into his father's favor. Now since Neil himself had so effectively reversed that trend, Buddy reasoned that it would be only a matter of time before he would again enjoy the privileges of his primogeniture. The extinction of the species (were Herefords a species?) was not too high a price to pay.

There was one other who rejoiced at this turn of events, but he was not, either in his own estimation or in theirs, one of the townspeople. Jeremiah Orville had hoped that Gracie or her calf or both might die, for the preservation of the cattle had been one of Anderson's proudest achievements, a token that civilization-as-we-had-known-it was not quite passé and a sign, for those who would see it, that Anderson was truly of the Elect. That the agency that would realize Orville's hopes should be the incompetence of the man's own son afforded Orville an almost esthetic pleasure: as though some tidy, righteous deity were assisting his revenge, scrupulous that the laws of poetic justice be observed. Orville was happy tonight, and he worked at the butchering with a quiet fury. From time to time, when he could not be seen, he swallowed a gobbet of raw beef—for he was as hungry as any man there. But he would starve willingly, if only he might see Anderson starve before him.

A peculiar noise, a windy sound but not the wind, caught his attention. It seemed familiar, but he couldn't place it. It was a sound that belonged to the city. Joel Stromberg, who was looking after the pigs, shouted: "Ah, hey!—there—whadaya——" Abruptly, Joel was metamorphosed into a pillar of fire.

Orville saw this no more distinctly than he had heard the sound preceding it, but without taking thought he hurled himself over a nearby snowbank. He rolled in the powdery snow till he was out of sight of everything—the carcasses, the other men, the pigsty. Everything but the flames rising from the burning sty. "Mr. Anderson!" he yelled. Terrified lest he lose his intended victim to the fires of the incendiaries, he crawled back to rescue the old man.

Three spherical bodies, each about five feet in diameter, floated just above the snow at the periphery of the flames. The men (with the exception of Anderson, who was crouched behind the flank of the dead cow, aiming his pistol at the nearest sphere) stood watching the blaze, as though bewitched. Spumes of steamy breath drifted from their open mouths.

"Don't waste bullets on armor plate, Mr. Anderson. Come on—

they'll fire the commonroom next. We've got to get the people out of there."

"Yes," Anderson agreed, but he did not move. Orville had to pull him away. In that moment of stuporous incapacity, Orville thought he saw in Anderson the seed of what Neil had become.

Orville entered the commonroom first. Since the walls were buttressed with great drifts of snow, none of them was yet aware of the blaze outside. They were, as they had been all evening, leaden with unhappiness. Several had already gotten into bed.

"Everybody—start getting your clothes on," Orville commanded in a voice as calm as authoritative. "Leave this room as quickly as possible by the kitchen door and run into the woods. Take anything with you that's at hand, but don't waste time looking for things. Don't wait for someone else to catch up. Quickly, now."

As many as had heard Orville looked dumbfounded. It was not for him to be giving orders.

"Quickly," Anderson directed, "and no questions."

They were accustomed to obeying Anderson unquestioningly, but there was still much confusion. Anderson, accompanied by Orville, went directly to the area by the kitchen where his own family was quartered. They were all bundling into their heavy clothes, but Anderson bundled them faster.

Outside there were screams, brief as the whistle of a slaughtered rabbit, as the incendiary devices were turned on their spectators. A man ran into the room, flaming, and fell to the floor, dead. The panic began. Anderson, already near the door, commanded respect even in the midst of hysteria and managed to get his family out among the first. Passing through the kitchen, Lady grabbed an empty cooking pot. Blossom was burdened with a basket of laundry, which, proving too heavy, she emptied into the snow. Orville, in his anxiety to see them out of the commonroom safely, took nothing at all. There were no more than fifty people running through the snow when the far corner of the commonroom caught fire. The first flames shot up thirty feet from the roof, then began to climb as they ate into the bags of corn stacked against the walls.

It is hard to run through unpacked snow, just as it is hard to run in knee-deep water: as soon as you acquire momentum, you are apt to tumble forward. Lady and Greta had left the house wearing only straw slippers, and others streamed out the door now in their nightshirts or wrapped in blankets.

The Andersons had almost reached the forest edge when Lady threw aside her cooking pot and exclaimed: *The Bible! the Bible is back there!*

No one heard her. She ran toward the burning building. By the time Anderson was aware of his wife's absence, there was no longer any way to stop her. His own scream would not be heard among so many others. The family stopped to watch. "Keep running," Orville shouted at them, but they paid no heed. Most of those who had escaped the house had reached the wood by now.

The flames illuminated the neighborhood of the building for a hundred feet, making the snow shine with an unsteady orange glow upon which the swift, uncertain shadows of the smoke rippled, like the fires of visible darkness.

Lady entered by the kitchen door and did not re-emerge. The roof caved in; the walls fell outward, neatly as dominos. The three spherical bodies could be seen in silhouette to rise higher from the ground. In close formation they began to glide toward the wood, their hum disguised by the crackling of the flames. Within the triangle they defined, the snow melted and bubbled and rose steaming into the air.

"Why would she do a thing like that?" Anderson asked of his daughter, but seeing that she was delicately poised on the brink of hysteria, he took her in one hand and the length of rope he had taken up from a wheelbarrow outside the house in the other and hurried after the others. Orville and Neil were practically carrying barefoot Greta, who was screaming obscenities in her rich contralto.

Orville was frantic, and yet close behind the frenzy was a sense of exultation and headlong delight that made him want to cheer, as though the conflagration behind them were as innocent and festal as a homecoming game bonfire.

When he shouted *Hurry on; hurry on!* it was hard to tell whether he was calling to Anderson and Blossom or to the three incendiaries not far behind them.

EIGHT **THE WAY DOWN**

Maybe we'll die, Maryann thought, when they had at last stopped running and she could think. But that was impossible. It was so cold! She wished to heaven she could understand what Anderson was talking about. He'd just said: "We'll have to take inventory." They were all standing around in the snow. It was so cold, and when she'd fallen down she'd gotten snow inside her coat, under her collar. The snow was still coming down in the dark. She'd catch a cold and then what would she do? Where would she live? And her baby—what about him?

"Maryann?" Anderson asked. "*She's* here, isn't she?"

"Maryann!" Buddy barked impatiently.

"I'm here," she said, snuffling the wet that trickled from her nose.

"Well—what did you bring with you?"

Each of her numb hands (she'd forgotten mittens too) was holding something, but she didn't know what. She held up her hands so she could see what was in them. "Lamps," she said. "The lamps from the kitchen, but one of them is broken. The chimney's smashed." It was only then that she remembered falling on it and cutting her knee.

"Who's got matches?" Orville asked.

Clay Kestner had matches. He lit the good lamp. By its light Anderson took a headcount: "Thirty-one." There was a long silence while each survivor examined the thirty other faces and tallied his own losses. There were eighteen men, eleven women and two children.

Mae Stromberg began to cry. She'd lost a husband and a daughter, though her son was with her. In the panic Denny had not been able to find the shoe for his left foot, and Mae had pulled him the three miles from the conflagration on one of the children's sleds. Anderson, having concluded the inventory, told Mae to be quiet.

"Maybe there'll be more food back there," Buddy was saying to his father. "Maybe it won't be burnt up so bad we can't still eat it."

"I doubt it," Orville said. "Those damn flamethrowers are pretty thorough."

"How long will what we've got last if we ration it?" Buddy asked.

"Till Christmas," Anderson replied curtly.

"If *we* last till Christmas," Orville said. "Those machines are probably scouting the woods now, picking off anyone who got out of the fire. There's also a matter of where we'll spend the night. Nobody thought to bring along tents."

"We'll go back to the old town," Anderson said. "We can stay in the church and tear off the siding for firewood. Does anyone know where we are now? Every goddam Plant in this forest looks like every other goddam Plant."

"I've got a compass," Neil volunteered. "I'll get us there. You just follow me." Off in the distance, there was a scream, a very brief scream. "I think it's that way," Neil said, moving toward the scream.

They formed a broad phalanx with Neil at the head and moved on through the snowy night. Orville pulled Greta along on the sled, and Buddy carried Denny Stromberg on his back.

"Can I hold your hand?" Maryann asked him. "Mine are just numb."

Buddy let her put her hand in his, and they walked along together for a half hour in perfect silence. Then he said, "I'm glad you're safe."

"Oh!" It was all she could say. Her nose was dripping like a leaky faucet, and she began to cry too. The tears froze on her cold cheeks. Oh, she was so happy!

They almost walked through the village without realizing it. An inch of snow had blanketed the cold, leveled ashes.

Denny Stromberg was the first to speak. "Where will we go now, Buddy? Where will we sleep?" Buddy didn't answer. Thirty people waited in silence for Anderson, who was kicking the ashes with the toe of his boot, to lead them through this Red Sea.

"We must kneel and pray," he said. "Here, in this church, we must kneel and ask forgiveness for our sins." Anderson knelt in the snow and ashes. "Almighty and merciful God . . ."

A figure came out of the woods, running, stumbling, breathless—a woman in bedclothes with a blanket wrapped shawl-like about her. Falling to her knees in the middle of the group, she could not draw breath to speak. Anderson ceased praying. In the direction from which she had come, the forest glowed faintly, as though, at a distance, a candle were burning in a farmhouse window.

"It's Mrs. Wilks," Alice Nemerov announced, and at the same moment Orville said, "We'd better pray somewhere else. That looks like a new fire over there."

"There *is* nowhere else," Anderson said.

"There must be," Orville insisted. Under the pressure of hours of crisis, he had lost track of his original motive—to save the Andersons for his personal revenge, for slower agonies. His desire was more primary—self-preservation. "If there are no houses left, there must still be someplace to hide: a burrow, a cave, a culvert . . ." Something he had said touched the chord of memory. A burrow? A cave?

"A cave! Blossom, a long time ago, when I was sick, you told me you'd been in a cave. You'd never seen a mine, but you'd been in a cave. Was that near here?"

"It's by the lake shore—the old lake shore. Near Stromberg's Resort. It's not far, but I haven't been in it since I was a little girl. I don't know if it's still there."

"How big a cave is it?"

"Very big. At least, I thought so then."

"Could you take us there?"

"I don't know. It's hard enough in the summertime to find your way around through the Plants. All the old landmarks are gone, and with the snow besides . . ."

"Take us there, girl! Now!" Anderson rasped. He was himself again, more or less.

They left the half-naked woman behind them lying in the snow. Not through cruelty: it was simply forgetfulness. When they had gone, the woman looked up and said, "Please." But the people whom she had thought to address were not there. Perhaps they had never been there. She got to her feet and dropped her blanket.

It was very cold. She heard the humming sound again and ran

blindly back into the woods, heading in the opposite direction from that which Blossom had taken.

The three incendiary spheres glided to the spot where the woman had lain, quickly converted the blanket there to ash, and moved on after Mrs. Wilks, following the spoor of blood.

Much of the old lake shore was still recognizable under the mantle of snow: the conformation of the rocks, the stairways going down to the water—they even found a post that had once been part of the resort's pier. From the pier Blossom estimated it would be a hundred yards to the cave entrance. She went along the rockface that rose ten feet above the old beach and played the lamplight into likely crevasses. Wherever she directed him, Buddy cleared the snow with a shovel, which, along with an axe, he had rescued from the commonroom. The other searchers scraped off the snow (which had drifted more than a yard deep among the boulders) with their hands, mittened or bare, as luck would have it.

The work went slowly, for Blossom remembered the entrance to the cave as being halfway up the rockface, so that one had to clamber over snowy rocks to be able to dig. Despite the hazard this involved, they did not have time to be careful. Behind the clouds, from which the snow sifted steadily down, there was no moon; the digging went on in near-total darkness. At regular intervals one of them would call a sudden halt to the work and they would stand there straining to hear the telltale hum of their pursuers that someone had thought he'd heard.

Blossom, under the unaccustomed weight of responsibility, became erratic, running from rock to rock. "Here!" she would say, and then, running: "Or here?" She was a good two hundred yards from the old pier, and Buddy began to doubt that there *was* a cave.

If there were not, then surely they had come to an end.

The prospect of death disturbed him most in that he could not grasp the *purpose* of these burnings. If this were an invasion (and even his father could not doubt that now; the Good Lord did not need to build machines to wreak his vengeance), what did the invaders want? Were the Plants themselves the invaders? No, no—they were only Plants.

One had to suppose that the real invaders—the ones inside the incendiary globes (or whoever had built them and put them to work)—wanted the Earth for no other reason than to grow their damn Plants. Was Earth, then, their farm? If so, why had there been no harvest?

It wounded his pride to think that his race, his species, his world was being defeated with such apparent ease. What was worse, what he could not endure was the suspicion that it all meant nothing, that the process of their annihilation was something quite mechanical: that mankind's destroyers were not, in other words, fighting a war but merely spraying the garden.

The opening to the cave was discovered inadvertently—Denny Stromberg fell through it. Without that happy chance, they might well have gone the whole night without finding it, for everyone in their party had passed it by.

The cave went farther back than the lamplight would reach from the entrance, but before the full depth was explored, everyone was inside. All the adults except Anderson, Buddy, and Maryann (all three under five feet six) had to bend over double or even crawl to keep from hitting their heads against the crumbling ceiling. Anderson declared that the moment for silent prayer was at hand, for which Orville was grateful. Huddled next to each other for warmth, their backs against the sloping wall of the cave, they tried to recover their sense of identity, of purpose, of touch—whatever senses they had lost in the hours-long stampede through the snow. The lamp was left burning, since Anderson judged that matches were more precious than oil.

After five minutes given over to prayers, Anderson, Buddy, Neil and Orville (though not of the family hierarchy, he *had* been the one to think of the cave—and of more things besides than Anderson cared to reckon) explored the back of the cave. It was big but not so big as they'd hoped, extending some twenty feet to the rear, narrowing continually. At its far end, there was a small el filled with bones.

"Wolves!" Neil declared.

Closer inspection confirmed this with some definiteness, for the skeletons of the wolves themselves were discovered, stripped as clean as the others, topmost on the pile.

"Rats," Neil decided. "Just rats."

To reach the far depth of the cave they had had to squeeze past the gigantic root of a Plant that had broken through the cave wall. Returning from the pile of bones the men examined this, the only other exceptional feature of the cave, with some care. The Plant's root at this level was very little distinguishable from its trunk. To judge from the curvature of the portion exposed in the cave, it was, like the bole of the Plant, some fourteen or fifteen feet in diameter. Near the floor of the cave, the smooth surface of the root was abraded, just as the smooth green trunks were often chewed by hungry rabbits. Here, however, there appeared to be more than a nibble taken out.

Orville stooped to examine it. "Rabbits didn't do this. It's gone right to the heart of the wood." He reached his hand into the dark hole. The outermost layer of wood extended no more than a foot, beyond which his fingers encountered what seemed a tangle of vines—and beyond this (his whole shoulder pressing against the hole), nothing; emptiness; air. "This thing is hollow!"

"Nonsense," Anderson said. He got down beside Orville and thrust his own arm into the hole. "It can't be," he said, feeling that it could be and was.

"Rabbits certainly didn't make *that* hole," Orville insisted.

"Rats," Neil repeated, more than ever confirmed in his judgment. But, as usual, no one paid him any attention.

"It *grows* that way. Like the stem of a dandelion—it's hollow."

"It's dead. Termites must have gotten to it."

"The only dead Plants I've seen, Mr. Anderson, are the ones we've killed. If you don't object, I'd like to see what's down there."

"I don't see what good that could do. You have an unhealthy curiosity about these Plants, young man. I sometimes have the impression that you're more on their side than on ours."

"The good it could do," Orville said, half-truthfully (for he dared not yet express his real hope), "is that it may provide a back door to the cave—an escape hatch to the surface in the event that we're followed here."

"He's right about that, you know," Buddy volunteered.

"I don't need your help to make up my mind. *Either* of you," Anderson added when he saw that Neil had begun to smile at this. "You are right again, Jeremiah . . ."

"Just call me Orville, sir. Everyone else does."

Anderson smiled acidly. "Yes. Well. Shall we start to work now? As I recall, one of the men managed to bring a hatchet. Oh, it was you, Buddy? Bring it here. Meanwhile, you—" (designating Orville) "—will see that everyone moves to the back of the cave, where they'll be warmer. And safer perhaps. Also, find some way to block up the entrance, so the snow will cover it over again. Use your coat if necessary."

When the opening to the root had been sufficiently enlarged, Anderson thrust the lamp in and squeezed his bony torso through. The cavity narrowed rapidly overhead, becoming no more than a tangle of vines; there was little possibility of an exit—at least not without much hard work. But *below* was an abyss that stretched quite beyond the weak shaft of light from the lamp. The lamp's effectiveness was further diminished by what seemed to be a network of gauze or cobweb that filled the hollow of the root. The light passing through this airy stuff was diffused and softened so that beyond a depth of fifteen feet one could discern only a formless, pinkish glow.

Anderson swiped at these strands of gauze, and they broke unresistingly. His calloused hand could not even feel them giving way.

Anderson squirmed back out of the narrow hole and into the cave proper. "Well, it won't be any use to escape by. It's solid up above. It goes *down,* though—farther than I can see. Look for yourself if you want."

Orville wormed into the hole. He stayed there so long, Anderson became annoyed. When he reappeared he was almost grinning. "That's where we'll go, Mr. Anderson. Why, it's perfect!"

"You're crazy," Anderson said matter-of-factly. "We're bad enough off where we are."

"But the point is—" (And this had been his original, unexpressed hope.) "—that it will be *warm* down there. Once you get fifty feet below the surface, it's always a comfortable fifty degrees Fahrenheit. There's no winter and no summer that deep in the ground. If you prefer it warmer than that just go down deeper. It warms up one degree for every sixty feet."

"Ah, what are you talking about?" Neil jeered. "That sounds like a lot of hooey." He didn't like the way Orville—a stranger—was telling them what to do all the time. He had no *right*!

"It's one thing I should know about, being a mining engineer. Isn't that why I'm alive, after all?" He let that sink in, then continued calmly: "One of the biggest problems in working deep mines is keeping them at a bearable temperature. The least we can do is see how far down it does go. It must be fifty feet at least—that would be only a tenth of its height."

"There's no soil fifty feet down," Anderson objected. "Nothing but rock. Nothing grows in rock."

"Tell that to the Plant. I don't know if it does go that deep, but again I say we should explore. We've a length of rope, and even if we didn't, those vines would support any of us. I tested them." He paused before he returned to the clinching argument: "If nothing else, it's a place to hide if those things find their way to us."

His last argument turned out as valid as it had been effective. Buddy had only just gone down by the rope to the first branching off of the secondary roots from the vertical primary root (Buddy had been chosen because he was the lightest of the men), when there was a grating sound at the entrance of the cave, as when children try to fill a glass bottle with sand. One of the spheres, having tracked them to the cave, was now trying to bulldoze its way through the narrow entrance.

"Shoot!" Neil yelled at his father. "Shoot it!" He started to grab for the Python in his father's side holster.

"I don't intend to waste good ammunition on armor plate. Now, get your hands off me and let's start pushing people down that hole."

Orville did not have to prompt any further. There was nothing left for them to do. Not a thing. They were the puppets of necessity now. He stood back from the melee and listened as the sphere tried to shove its way into the cave by main force. In some ways, he thought, those spheres were no smarter than a chicken trying to scratch its way through a wire fence that it could walk around. Why not just shoot? Perhaps the three spheres had to be grouped about their target before they could go zap. They were, almost surely, automatons. They directed their own destinies no more than did the animals they were programmed to track down. Orville had no sympathy for the dumb machines and none for their prey. He rather fancied himself at that moment as the puppeteer, until the real puppeteer, necessity, twitched a finger, and Orville went running after his fellow men.

————

The descent into the root was swift and efficient. The size of the hole insured that no more than one person passed through at a time, but fear insured that that person got through as fast as he could. The unseen (the lamp was below with Buddy) presence of the metal sphere grinding at the ceiling and walls of the cave was a strong motivation to speed.

Anderson made each person strip off his bulky outer clothing and push it through the hole ahead of him. At last only Anderson, Orville, Clay Kestner, Neil and Maryann were left. It was evident that for Clay and Neil (the largest men of the village) and for Maryann, now in her eighth month, the hole would have to be enlarged. Neil chopped at the pulpy wood with frantic haste and much wasted effort. Maryann was eased first through the expanded opening. When she reached her husband, who was astraddle the inverse v formed by the divergence of the branch root from the greater taproot, her hands were raw from having slipped down the rope too quickly. As soon as he laid hold of her, all her strength seemed to leave her body. She could not go on. Neil was the next to descend, then Clay Kestner. Together they carried Maryann on into the secondary root.

Anderson called out, "Watch out below!" and a steady rain of objects—foodstuffs, baskets, pots, clothing, the sled, whatever the people had brought with them from the fire—fell into the abyss, shattering the delicate traceries. Buddy tried to count the seconds between the time they were released and the moment they hit bottom, but after a certain point he could not distinguish between the sounds of the objects ricocheting off the walls of the root and their striking bottom, if any. Anderson descended the rope after the last of the provisions had been dropped down the root.

"How is Orville coming down?" Buddy asked. "Who'll hold the rope for him?"

"I didn't bother to ask. Where is everyone else?"

"Down there . . ." Buddy gestured vaguely into the blackness of the secondary root. The lamp was lighting the main shaft, where the descent was more dangerous. The secondary root diverged at a forty-five degree angle from its parent. The ceiling (for here there could be said to be floor and ceiling) rose to a height of seven feet. The entire surface of the root was a tangle of vines, so that the slope was easy to negotiate. The interior space had been webbed with the same fragile lace, though those who had preceded Anderson into the root had broken most of it away.

Orville clambered down on the vines, the end of the rope knotted about his waist in the manner of a mountain climber. An unnecessary precaution, as it proved: the vines—or whatever they were—held firm. They were almost rigid, in fact, from being so closely knit together.

"Well," said Orville, in a voice grotesque with good cheer, "here's everybody, safe and sound. Shall we go down to the basement, where the groceries are?"

At that moment he felt an almost godlike elation, for he had held Anderson's life in his hands—literally, by a string—and it had been his to decide whether the old man should die just then or suffer yet a little longer. It had not been a difficult choice, but, ah, it had been *his!*

NINE THE WORM SHALL FEED SWEETLY

When they had ventured down the branch root a further twenty-five feet (where, as Orville had promised, it was tolerably warm), they reached a sort of crossroads. There were three new branches to choose from, each as commodious as the one through which they had been traveling. Two descended, like proper roots, though veering off perpendicularly to the right and left of their parent; the other shot steeply upward.

"That's strange," Buddy observed. "Roots don't grow up."

"How do you know that's up?" Orville asked.

"Well, look at it. It's *up*. Up is . . . up. It's the opposite of down."

"My point exactly. We're *looking* up the root, which may be *growing* down to us—from another Plant perhaps."

"You mean this thing could be just one big Plant?" Anderson asked, moving into the circle of lamplight, scowling. He resented each further attribute of the Plant, even those that served his purpose. "All of them linking up together down here this way?"

"There's one sure way to find out, sir—follow it. If it takes us to another primary root—"

"We don't have time to be Boy Scouts. Not until we've found the supplies we dropped down that hole. Will we get to them this way? Or will we have to backtrack and climb down the main root on the rope?"

"I couldn't say. This way is easier, faster and, for the moment, safer. If the roots join up like this regularly, maybe we can find another way back to the main root farther down. So I'd say—"

"I'll say," Anderson said, repossessing, somewhat, his authority. Buddy was sent ahead with the lamp and one end of the rope; the thirty others followed after, Indian file. Anderson and Orville bringing up the rear had only the sounds of the advance party to guide them: both the light and the rope were played out this far back.

But there was a plenitude of sound: the shuffle of feet over the vines, men swearing, Denny Stromberg crying. Every so often Greta inquired of the darkness: "Where are we?" or "Where the hell *are* we?" But that was only one noise among many. There were, already, a few premonitory sneezes, but they went unnoticed. The thirty-one people moving through the root were still rather shell-shocked. The rope they held to was at once their motive and their will.

Anderson kept stumbling on the vines. Orville put an arm around the old man's waist to steady him. Anderson tore it loose angrily. "You think I'm some kind of invalid?" he said. "Get the hell out of here!"

But the next time he stumbled, he went headlong into the rough vines of the floor, scratching his face. Rising, he had a dizzy spell and would have fallen again without Orville's help. Despite himself, he felt a twinge of gratitude for the arm that bore him up. In the darkness, he couldn't see that Orville was smiling.

Their path wound on down through the root, passing two more intersections such as the one above. Both times Buddy turned left, so that their descent described, approximately, a spiral. The hollow of the root gave no sign of diminishing; if anything it had been growing larger for the last few yards. There was no danger of becoming lost, for the shattering of the root's lacy interior blazed an unmistakable trail through the labyrinth.

A commotion at the head of the line brought them to a halt. Anderson and Orville pushed their way to the front.

Buddy handed the lamp to his father. "It's a dead end," he announced. "We'll have to go back the way we came."

The root's hollow was much enlarged at this point, and the cobwebby stuff filling it more condensed. Instead of shattering glassily under the force of Anderson's blow, it tore off in handfuls, like rotted fabric. Anderson pressed one of these pieces between his hands. Like the pink candy floss at carnivals or like the airiest kind of white bread, it wadded into a little ball less than an inch round.

"We'll push our way through," Anderson announced. He took a step back, then threw his shoulder like a football tackle into the yielding floss. His momentum gave out two and a half yards ahead. Then, because there was nothing solid beneath his feet, he began, slowly, to sink out of sight. Inexorably, under his weight, the candy floss gave way. Buddy stretched his hand forward, and Anderson was able barely to catch hold, fingertips hooked in fingertips. Anderson pulled Buddy into the mire with him. Buddy, falling in a horizontal position, served somewhat as a parachute, and they sank more slowly and came to a stop, safely, some ten feet below.

As they fell, a powerful sweetness, like the odor of rotting fruit, filled the air behind them.

Orville was the first to realize their good fortune. He wadded a mass of the floss to medium density and bit into it. The Plant's characteristic anise flavor could be discerned, but there was besides a fullness and sweetness, a satisfaction, that was quite new. His tongue recognized it before his mind did and craved another taste. No, not just his tongue—his belly. Every malnourished cell of his body craved more.

"Throw us down the rope," Anderson shouted hoarsely. He was not hurt, but he was shaken.

Instead of playing out the rope, Orville, with a happy, carefree shout, dove into the flossy mass. As he was swallowed into its darkness, he addressed the old man below: "Your prayers have been answered, sir. You've led us across the Red Sea, and now the Lord is feeding us manna. Taste the stuff—taste it! We don't have to worry about those supplies. This is the reason for the Plants. This is their fruit. This is manna from heaven."

In the brief stampede over the edge, Mae Stromberg sprained her ankle. Anderson knew better than to pit his authority against raw hunger. He hesitated to eat the fruit himself, for it could be poisonous, but his body's need strained against an overcautious will. If the rest of them were to be poisoned, he might as well join them.

It tasted good.

Yes, he thought, *it must seem like manna to them.* And even as the sugary floss condensed on his tongue into droplets of honey, he hated the Plant for seeming so much their friend and their deliverer. For making its poison so delicious.

At his feet the lamp burned unnaturally bright. The floor, though hard enough to hold him up, was not rock-solid. He took out his pocket knife, brushed away the matted floss, and cut a slice of this more solid substance from the fruit. It was crisp, like an Idaho potato, and juicy. It had a blander and less acid taste than the floss. He cut out another piece. He could not stop eating.

Around Anderson, out of range of the lamp, the citizens of Tassel (but was there still a Tassel of which they could be said to be citizens?) snuffled and ate like swine at a trough. Most of them did not bother to press the floss into comfortable mouthfuls but pushed it blindly into their mouths, biting their own fingers and gagging in their greedy haste. Strands of the pulp adhered to their clothes and tangled in their hair. It stuck to the lashes of their closed eyes.

An upright figure advanced into the sphere of lamplight. It was Jeremiah Orville. "I'm sorry," he said, "if I started all this. I shouldn't have spoken out of turn. I should have waited for you to say what to do. I wasn't thinking."

"That's all right," Anderson assured him, his mouth full of half-chewed fruit. "It would have happened the same no matter what you did. Or what I did."

Orville sat down beside the older man. "In the morning . . ." he began.

"Morning? It must be morning now." In fact, they had no way to know. The only working timepieces—an alarm clock and two wristwatches—had been kept in a box in the commonroom for safety. No one escaping the fire had thought to rescue the box.

"Well, when everyone's fed full and they've got some sleep—that's what I meant—then you can set them to work. We've lost a battle, but there's still a war to fight."

Orville's tone was politely optimistic, but Anderson found it oppressive. To have come to sanctuary after a disaster did not erase the memory of the disaster. Indeed, Anderson, now that he had stopped running from it, was only just becoming aware of its magnitude. "What work?" he asked, spitting out the rest of the fruit.

"Whatever work you say, sir. Exploring. Clearing out a space down here to live in. Going back to the main root for the supplies we dropped there. Pretty soon, you might even send a scout back to see if anything can be salvaged from the fire."

Anderson made no reply. Sullenly he recognized that Orville was right. Sullenly he admired his resourcefulness, just as, twenty years earlier, he might have admired an opponent's fighting style in a brawl at Red Fox Tavern. Though to Anderson's taste the style was a little too fancy, you had to give the bastard credit for keeping on his feet.

It was strange, but Anderson's whole body was tensed as though for a fight, as though he *had* been drinking.

Orville was saying something. "*What'd* you say?" Anderson asked in a jeering tone. He hoped it was something that would give him an excuse to smash his face in, the smart punk.

"I said—I'm very sorry about your wife. I can't understand why she did that. I know how you must be feeling."

Anderson's fists unclenched, his jaw grew slack. He felt the pressure of tears behind his eyes, the pressure that had been there all along, but he knew that he could not afford to give in to it. He could not afford the least weakness now.

"Thank you," he said. Then he cut out another large wedge of the solider, more succulent fruit, split it into two, and gave part to Jeremiah Orville. "You've done well tonight," he said. "I will not forget it."

Orville left him to whatever thoughts he had and went looking for Blossom. Anderson, alone, thought of his wife with a stony, dumb grief. He could not understand why she had, as he considered it, committed suicide.

He would never know, no one would know, that she had turned back for his sake. He had not yet taken thought of the Bible that had been left behind, and later, when he would, he would regret it no more nor less than Gracie's death or the hundred other irredeemable losses he had suffered. But Lady had foreseen quite accurately that without that one artifact, in which she herself had had no faith, without the sanction it lent his authority, the old man would be bereft, and that his strength, so long preserved, would soon collapse, like a roof when the timbers have rotted. But she had failed, and her failure would never be understood.

More than one appetite demanded satisfaction that night. A satiety of food produced, in men and women alike, an insatiable hunger for that which the strict code of the commonroom had so long denied them. Here, in warmth and darkness, that code no longer obtained. In its stead, the perfect democracy of the carnival proclaimed itself, and liberty reigned for one brief hour.

Hands brushed, as though by accident, other hands—exactly whose it made little difference. Death had not scrupled to sort out husband and wife, and neither did they. Tongues cleaned away the sweet, sticky film from lips that had done feasting, met other tongues, kissed.

"They're drunk," Alice Nemerov stated unequivocally.

She, Maryann and Blossom sat in a separate cove dug from the pulp of the fruit, listening, trying not to listen. Though each couple tried to observe a decorous silence, the cumulative effect was unmistakable, even to Blossom.

"Drunk? How can that be?" Maryann asked. She did not want to talk, but conversation was the only defense against the voluptuous sounds of the darkness. Talking and listening to Alice talk, she did not have to hear the sighing, the whispers—or wonder which was her husband's.

"We're all drunk, my dears. Drunk on oxygen. Even with this stinking fruit stinking things up, I know an oxygen tent when I smell it."

"I don't smell anything," Maryann said. It was perfectly true: her cold had reached the stage where she couldn't even smell the cloying odor of the fruit.

"I worked in a hospital, didn't I? So I should know. My dears, we're all of us higher than kites."

"High as the flag on the Fourth of July," Blossom put in. She didn't really mind being drunk, if it was like this. Floating. She wanted to sing but sensed that it wasn't the thing to do. Not now. But the song, once begun, kept on inside her head: *I'm in love, I'm in love, I'm in love, I'm in love, I'm in love with a wonderful guy.*

"Sssh!" Alice ssshed.

"Excuse *me!*" Blossom said, with a wee giggle. Perhaps her song had not after all been altogether inside her head. Then, because she knew it was the correct thing to do when tipsy, she hiccoughed a single, graceful hiccough, fingertips pressed delicately to her lips. Then, indelicately, she burped, for there was gas on her stomach.

"Are you all right, my dear?" Alice asked, laying a solicitous hand on Maryann's full womb. "I mean, everything that's happened——"

"Yes. There, you see! He just moved."

The conversation lapsed, and through the breach the assault was renewed. Now it was an angry, persistent sound, like the buzzing of a honeycomb. Maryann shook her head, but the buzzing wouldn't stop. "Oh!" she gasped. "Oh!"

"There, there," Alice soothed.

"Who do you think is with him?" Maryann blurted.

"Why, you're all upset for no reason at all," Blossom said. "He's probably with Daddy and Orville this very minute."

Blossom's obvious conviction almost swayed Maryann. It *was* possible. An hour ago (or less? or more?) Orville had sought out Blossom and explained that he was taking her father (who was naturally very upset) to a more private spot, away from the others. He had found a way into another root, a root that burrowed yet deeper into the earth. Did Blossom want to go there with him? Or perhaps she preferred to stay with the ladies?

Alice had thought that Blossom would prefer to stay with the ladies for the time being. She would join her father later, if he wished her to.

Anderson's departure, and the departure with him of the lamp, had been the cue for all that followed. A month's dammed energy spilled out and covered, for a little while, the face of sorrow, blotted out the too-clear knowledge of their defeat and of an ignominy the features of which were only just becoming apparent.

A hand reached out of the darkness and touched Blossom's thigh. It was Orville's hand! It could be no other. She took the hand and pressed it to her lips.

It was not Orville's hand. She screamed. Instantly, Alice had caught the intruder by the scruff of his neck. He yelped.

"Neil!" she exclaimed. "For pity's sake! That's your sister you're pawing, you idiot! Now, *get*! Go look for Greta. Or, on the other hand, maybe you'd better not."

"You shut up!" Neil bellowed. "You ain't my mother!"

She finally shoved Neil away. Then she laid her head down in Blossom's lap. "Drunk," she scolded sleepily. "Absolutely stoned." Then she began to snore. In a few minutes, Blossom slept too—and dreamed—and woke with a little cry.

"What is it?" Maryann asked.

"Nothing, a dream," Blossom said. "Haven't you gone to sleep yet?"

"I can't." Though it was as quiet as death now, Maryann was still listening. What she feared most was that Neil *would* find his wife. And Buddy. Together.

Buddy woke. It was still dark. It would always be dark now, here. There was a woman beside him, whom he touched, though not to wake her. Assured that she was neither Greta nor Maryann, he gathered his clothes and sidled away. Strands of the sticky pulp caught on his bare back and shoulders and melted there, unpleasantly.

He was still feeling drunk. Drunk and drained. Orville had a word for the feeling—what was it?

Detumescent.

The grainy liquid trickled down his bare skin, made him shiver. But it wasn't that he was cold. Though he was cold, come to think of it.

Crawling forward on hands and knees, he bumbled into another sleeping couple. "What?" the woman said. She sounded like Greta. No matter. He crawled elsewhere.

He found a spot where the pulp had not been disturbed and shoved his body into it backward. Once you got used to the sticky feeling, it was quite comfortable: soft, warm, snuggly.

He wanted light: sunlight, lamplight, even the red, unsteady light of last night's burning. Something in the present situation horrified him in a way he did not understand, could not define. It was more than the darkness. He thought about it and as he dropped off to sleep again it came to him:

Worms.

They were worms, crawling through an apple.

TEN **FALLING TO PIECES**

W ho's *your* favorite movie star, Blossom?" Greta asked.

"Audrey Hepburn. I only saw her in one movie—when I was nine years old—but she was wonderful in that. Then there weren't any more movies. Daddy never approved, I guess."

"Daddy!" Greta snorted. She tore off a strand of fruit pulp from the space overhead, lowered it lazily into her mouth, mashed it with her tongue against the back of her teeth. Sitting in that pitch-black cavity in the fruit, her listeners could not see her do this, but it was evident from her blurred speech that she was eating again. "And you, Neil? Who's your favorite?"

"Charlton Heston. I used to go to anything with him in it."

"Me too," said Clay Kestner. "Him—and how about Marilyn *Mon*-roe? Any of you fellas old enough to remember old Marilyn *Mon*-roe?"

"Marilyn Monroe was vastly overrated in my opinion," Greta mouthed.

"What do you say about that, Buddy? Hey, Buddy! Is he still here?"

"Yeah, I'm still here. I never saw Marilyn Monroe. She was before my time."

"Oh, you missed something, kid. You really missed something."

"*I* saw Marilyn Monroe," Neil put in. "She wasn't before my time."

"And you still say Charlton Heston's your favorite?" Clay Kestner had a booming, traveling-salesman's laugh, gutsy and graceless. In former years he had been half-owner of a filling station.

"Oh, I don't know," Neil said nervously.

Greta laughed too, for Clay had begun to tickle her toes. "You're all wet, all of you," she said, still giggling but trying to stop. "I still say that Kim Novak is the greatest actress who ever lived." She had been saying it and saying it for fifteen minutes, and it seemed now that she would say it again.

Buddy was mortally bored. He had thought it would be better to stay behind with the younger set than to go along on another of his father's tedious, purposeless explorations through the labyrinthine roots of the Plants. Now that the supplies had been gathered in, now that they had learned everything about the Plant that there was to learn, there was no point in wandering about. And no point in sitting still. He had not realized till now, till there was nothing to do, what a slave to work and Puritan busy-ness he had become.

He rose, and his hair (cut short now, like everyone else's) brushed against the clinging fruit. The fruit pulp, when it dried and matted in one's hair, was more aggravating than a mosquito bite that couldn't be itched.

"Where are you going?" Greta asked, offended that her audience should desert her in the middle of her analysis of Kim Novak's peculiar charm.

"I've got to throw up," Buddy said. "See you all later."

It was a plausible enough excuse. The fruit, though it nourished them, had minor side effects. They were all, a month later (such was the estimate on which they had agreed), still suffering from diarrhea, gas pains and belly-aches. Buddy almost might have wished he did have to vomit: it would have been something to do.

Worse than the stomach upsets had been the colds. Nearly everyone had suffered from these too, and there had been no remedy but patience, sleep and a will to recover. In most cases these remedies were sufficient, but three cases of pneumonia had developed, Denny Stromberg among them. Alice Nemerov did what she could do, but as she was the first to confess, she could do nothing.

Buddy climbed up the rope from the tuber into the root proper. Here he had to walk crouched, for the hollow space in the root was only four and a half feet in diameter. Bit by bit over the last month, the party had moved down many hundreds of feet—to a depth, Orville had estimated, of at least 1,200 feet. Why, the Alworth Building wasn't that high. Not even the Foshay Tower in Minneapolis! At this depth the temperature was a relaxed seventy degrees.

There was a rustling sound close ahead. "Who's that?" Buddy and Maryann asked, almost in unison.

"What are you doing here?" Buddy asked his wife in a surly tone.

"Making more rope—but don't ask my why. It's just something to do. It keeps me busy. I've shredded up some of the vines, and now I'm putting them back together." She laughed weakly. "The vines were probably stronger than my ropes."

"Here, take my hands—show them how to do it."

"You!" When Buddy's hands touched hers, she continued busily knitting so that her fingers would not tremble. "Why would you want to do that?"

"As you say—it's something to do."

She began to guide his clumsy fingers but grew confused trying to keep in mind that his right hand was in her left and vice versa. "Maybe if I sat behind you . . ." she suggested. But as it turned out, she couldn't even close her arms around his chest. Her belly was in the way.

"How is he?" Buddy asked. "Will it be much longer?"

"He's fine. It should be any day now."

It worked out as she had hoped: Buddy sat behind her, his thighs clenched about her spread legs, his hairy arms beneath hers, supporting them like the armrests of a chair. "So teach me," he said.

He was a slow learner, not used to this kind of work, but his slowness only made him a more interesting pupil. They wore away an hour or more before he was ready to start his own rope. When he had finished it, the fibers fell apart like shreds of tobacco sliding out of a beginner's cigarette.

From deep inside the tuber came the music of Greta's laugh, and then Clay's bass-drum accompaniment. Buddy had no desire to rejoin them. He had no desire to go anywhere except back to the surface, its fresh air, its radiance, its changing seasons.

Maryann apparently was having similar thoughts. "Do you suppose it's Ground Hog's Day yet?"

"Oh, I'd say another week. Even if we were up there where we could see whether or not the sun was out, I doubt there'd be any groundhogs left to go looking for their shadows."

"Then Blossom's birthday could be today. We should remind her."

"How old is she now? Thirteen?"

"You'd better not let her hear that. She's fourteen and very emphatic about it."

Another sound came out of the fruit: a woman's anguished cry. Then a silence, without echoes. Buddy left Maryann on the instant to find out what had caused it. He returned shortly. "It's Mae Stromberg. Her Denny's dead. Alice Nemerov's taking care of her now."

"Pneumonia?"

"That, and he hasn't been able to hold any food."

"Ah, the poor thing."

The Plant was very efficient. In fact, as plants go, it couldn't be beat. It had already proved that. The more you learned about it, the more you had to admire it. If you were the sort to admire such things.

Consider its roots, for instance. They were hollow. The roots of comparable, Earth-evolved plants (a redwood is roughly comparable) are solid and woody throughout. But what for? The bulk of such roots is functionless; in effect, it is so much dead matter. A root's only job is to transport water and minerals up to the leaves and, when they've been synthesized into food, to carry them back down again. To accomplish this, a root must hold itself rigid enough to withstand the constant pressure of the soil and rock around it. All these things the Plant did excellently well—better, considering its dimensions, than the most efficient of Earth's own plants.

The greater open space within the root allowed the passage of more water, more quickly and farther. The tracheids and vessels that conduct water up through an ordinary root do not have a tenth of the capacity of the expansible capillaries that were the cobwebs of the Plant. Similarly, the vines lining the hollow roots could in a single day transport tons of liquid glucose and other materials from the leaves down to the tubers of fruit and the still-growing roots at the lowest levels. These were to the phloem of ordinary plants as an intercontinental pipeline is to a garden hose. The hollow space within the root served a further purpose: it supplied the nethermost regions of the Plant with air. These roots, stretching so far below the airy topsoil, did not have, as other roots would, an independent supply of oxygen. It had to be brought to them. Thus, from the tips of its leaves to the farthest rootcaps, the Plant *breathed*. It was this multifarious capacity for rapid and large-scale transportation that had accounted for the Plant's inordinate rate of growth.

The Plant was economical; it wasted nothing. As its roots sank deeper and thickened, the Plant digested even itself, forming thereby the hollow in which the complex network of capillaries and vines then took shape. The wood that was no longer needed to maintain a rigid exoskeleton was broken down into useful food.

But the fundamental economy of the Plant, its final excellence, consisted in none of these partial features, but rather in the fact that all Plants were one Plant. As certain insects have, by social organization, achieved that which to their individual members would have been impossible, so the separate Plants, by forming a single, indivisible whole, had heightened their effective power exponentially. Materials that were not available to one might be available to another in superfluity. Water, minerals, air, food—all were shared in the spirit of true communism: from each according to his ability, to each according to his need. The resources of an entire continent were at its disposal; it did not want for much.

The mechanism by which the socialization of the individual Plants took place was very simple. As soon as the first branch roots budded from the vertical primary root, they moved by a sort of mutual tropism toward the kindred branch roots of other Plants. When they met, they merged. When they had merged indissolubly, they diverged, seeking still another union at a deeper level. The many became one.

You had to admire the Plant. It was really a very beautiful thing, if you looked at it objectively, as, say, Jeremiah Orville looked at it.

Of course, it had had advantages other plants hadn't had. It had not had to evolve all by itself. It was also very well cared for.

Even so, there were pests. But that was being looked after. This was, after all, only its first season on Earth.

By the time Anderson, Orville and the other men (those who'd bothered to come) returned from that day's exploration deeper into the Plant, Mae Stromberg had already disappeared. So had her son's corpse. In her last hours with the dying boy, she had not said a word or wept a tear, and when he died there had been only that single maddened outcry. The loss of her husband and daughter she had borne much less calmly; she had felt, perhaps, that she could afford to lose them—could afford, therefore, to grieve for them afterwards. Grieving is a luxury. Now she was left only grief.

There were twenty-nine people, not counting Mae Stromberg. Anderson called for an assembly right away. Of the twenty-nine, only the two women still down with pneumonia and Alice Nemerov were absent.

"I am afraid," Anderson began, after a short prayer, "that we are falling to pieces." There was some coughing and a shuffle of feet. He waited for it to pass, then continued: "I can't blame anyone here for Mae's running off like this. I can't very well blame Mae either. But those of us who have been spared this last blow and guided here by Divine Providence, those of us, that is to say . . ."

He stopped, irretrievably tangled in his own words—something that had been happening to him increasingly of late. He pressed a hand to his forehead and drew a deep breath.

"What I mean to say is this: We can't just lay around eating milk and honey. There is work to be done. We must strengthen ourselves for the trials ahead, and. . . . And, that is to say, we must not let ourselves go *soft*.

"Today I have gone down lower into these infernal tunnels, and I found out that the fruit down there is better. Smaller and firmer— there's less of this sugar candy. I also found that there's less of this oxygen, which has been . . . I mean to say that up here we're turning into a bunch of—what was that word?"

"Lotus-eaters," Orville said.

"A bunch of lotus-eaters. Exactly. Now this must *stop*——" He struck his palm with his clenched fist in emphasis.

Greta, who had had her hand up during the latter half of this speech, at last spoke up without waiting for recognition. "May I ask a question?"

"What is it, Greta?"

"*What* work? I just don't see what it is that we've been neglecting."

"Well, we haven't been doing *any* work, girl. That's plain to see."

"That doesn't answer my question."

Anderson was aghast at this effrontery—and from *her*. Two months ago he could have had her stoned as an adultress—and now the harlot was vaunting her pride and rebellion for everyone to see.

He should have answered her challenge with a blow. He should have quelled that pride by letting it be known, even now, just what she was: a harlot—and with her husband's brother. That he did not return her attack was a weakness, and everyone could see that too.

After a long boding silence, he returned to his speech as though there had been no interruption. "We've got to get the lead out! We can't *lay around* like this. We'll keep on the move from now on. Every day. We won't sit around in one place. We'll *explore*."

"There's nothing *to* explore, Mr. Anderson. And *why* should we move every day? Why not clear out one space that's comfortable and live there? There's enough food in just one of these big potatoes——"

"Enough! That's enough, Greta! I've said all I'm going to. Tomorrow we——"

Greta stood up, but instead of moving forward into the lamplight, she backed away. "It is *not* enough! I've had enough of *you*. I'm sick and tired of being ordered around like I was a slave. I've had *enough* of it, I'm through! Mae Stromberg did the right thing when she——"

"Sit down, Greta," the old man ordered, his sternness breaking into mere stridency. "Sit down and shut up."

"Not me. Not Greta. Not any more. I'm going. I have had it. From now on, I do as I damn well please, and anyone that wants to come along is welcome."

Anderson drew his pistol and pointed it at the shadowy figure outside of the lamp's full light. "Neil, you tell your wife to sit down. If she don't I'll shoot her. And I'll shoot to kill—by *God* I will!"

"Uh, sit down, Greta," Neil urged.

"You won't shoot me—and do you want to know why you won't shoot me? Because I'm pregnant. You wouldn't kill your own grandchild, now would you? And there's no doubt he *is* your grandchild."

It was a lie, a complete fabrication, but it served its purpose.

"My grandchild?" Anderson echoed, aghast. "My *grandchild*!" He turned his Python on Buddy. His hand trembled—with rage or simply with infirmity, one could not tell.

"It wasn't me," Buddy blurted. "I swear it wasn't me."

Greta had disappeared into the darkness, and three men were scrambling to their feet, eager to follow her. Anderson shot four bullets into the back of one of the men. Then, utterly spent, senseless, he collapsed over the feebly burning lamp. It was extinguished.

The man he had killed was Clay Kestner. The fourth bullet, passing through Clay's chest, had entered the brain of a woman who had leapt up in panic at Anderson's first shot.

There were now twenty-four of them, not counting Greta and the two men who had gone off with her.

ELEVEN A NATURAL DEATH

Anderson's hair was coming out in handfuls. Maybe it would have at his age in any case, but he blamed it on his diet. The supplies rescued from the fire had been rationed out in dribs and drabs, and the little corn that remained now was for Maryann and for seed when they returned to the surface.

He scratched at his flaky scalp and cursed the Plant, but it was a half-hearted curse—as though he were peeved with an employer, instead of at war with an enemy. His hatred had become tainted with gratitude; his strength was quitting him.

More and more he pondered the question of who was to succeed him. It was a weighty question: Anderson was perhaps the last leader in the world—a king almost, undoubtedly a patriarch.

Though generally he believed in primogeniture, he wondered if a difference of only three months might not be construed charitably in favor of the younger son. He refused to think of Neil as a bastard, and he had therefore been obliged to treat the boys as twins—impartially.

There was something to be said for each of them—and not enough for either. Neil was a steady worker, not given to complainings, and strong; he had the instincts of a leader of men, if not all the abilities.

However, he was stupid: Anderson could not help but see it. He was also . . . well, disturbed. Just how he was disturbed or why, Anderson did not know, though he suspected that Greta was in some way responsible. Considering this problem, he tended to be vague, to eye it obliquely or as through smoked glass, as we are told to observe an eclipse. He did not want to learn the truth if he could help it.

Buddy, on the other hand, though he possessed many of the qualities lacking in his half-brother, was not to be relied upon. He had proven it when, in the face of his father's sternest disapproval, he had gone to live in Minneapolis; he had proven it conclusively on Thanksgiving Day. When Anderson had found his son in, as he supposed, the very commission of the act, it had become quite clear that Buddy would not succeed to his own high place. Anderson, in passing from early manhood to middle age, had developed an unreasoning horror of adultery. That he had once been adulterate himself and that one of his children was the fruit of such a union did not occur to him now. He would, in fact, have denied it outright—and he would have believed his denial.

For a long time it had seemed that no one could possibly take his place. Therefore, he would have to carry on alone. Each time his sons had shown new weaknesses, Anderson had felt a corresponding growth in strength and purpose. Secretly, he had thrived on their failings.

Then Jeremiah Orville had entered the scene. In August, Anderson had been moved by reasons which were obscure and (it now seemed) God-given to spare the man. Today he trembled at his sight—as Saul must have trembled when he first realized that young David would supplant him and his son Jonathan. Anderson tried desperately both to deny this and to accommodate himself to his apparent heir. (He constantly feared that he would, like that earlier king, war against the Lord's annointed and damn himself in the act. Belief in predestination has decidedly some disadvantages.) As by degrees, he bent his will to this unpleasant task (for, though he admired Orville, he did not like him); his strength and purpose quitted him by equal degrees. Orville, without even knowing it, was killing him.

It was night. That is to say, they had once again journeyed to exhaustion. As Anderson was the arbiter of what constituted exhaustion, it was evident to everyone that the old man was being worn down: as after the vernal equinox, each day was shorter than the day that had gone before.

The old man scratched at his flaky scalp, and cursed . . . something, he couldn't remember exactly what, and fell asleep without thinking to take a count of heads. Orville, Buddy and Neil each took the count for him. Orville and Buddy both arrived at twenty-four. Neil, somehow, had come up with twenty-six.

"But that's not possible," Buddy pointed out.

Neil was adamant: he had counted twenty-six. "Whadaya think—I can't *count,* for Christ's sake?"

Since Greta's departure, a month or so had gone by. No one was keeping track of the time any longer. Some maintained it was February; others held for March. From the expeditions to the surface they knew only that it was still winter. They needed to know no more than that.

Not everyone went along. Indeed, besides Anderson, his two sons and Orville, there were only three other men. A permanent base of operations was again being maintained for those, like Maryann and Alice, who could not spend the day crawling through the roots. The number of those who deemed themselves incapable had grown daily until there were just as many lotus-eaters as before. Anderson pretended to ignore the situation, fearing to provoke a worse one.

Anderson led the men up by the usual route, which was marked by ropes that Maryann had braided. It was no longer possible for them to find their way about by the Ariadne's thread of broken capillaries, for in their explorations they had broken so many that they had created a labyrinth of their own.

It was near the surface, at about the sixty-degree level, that they came across the rats. At first it was like the humming of a beehive, though higher pitched. The men's first thought was that the incendiaries had at last come down into the roots after them. When they had ventured into the tuber from which the noise was coming, the humming rose to a raspy whine, as though a coloratura's aria were being broadcast at peak volume over a bad public-address system. The solid-seeming darkness beyond the lamp's reach wavered and dissolved to a lighter shade as thousands of rats tumbled over each other to get into the fruit. The walls of the passage were honeycombed with the rats' tunnelings.

"Rats!" Neil exclaimed. "didn't I say it was rats that gnawed their way through that root up above? Didn't I, huh? Well, here they are. There must be a million of them."

"If there aren't now, there will be before very long," Orville agreed. "I wonder if they're all in this one tuber?"

"What possible difference can it make?" Anderson asked impatiently. "They've left *us* well enough alone, and I for one feel no need to keep them company. They seem content to eat this damn candied apple, and I'm content to let them eat it. They can eat the whole of it, of all of them, for all I care." Sensing that he had gone too far, he said, in a more subdued tone: "There's nothing we can do against an army of rats, in any case. I have only one cartridge left in the revolver. I don't know what I'm saving it for, but I know it isn't for a rat."

"I was thinking of the future, Mr. Anderson. With all this food available and no natural enemies to keep them down, these rats will multiply out of all bounds. They may not threaten our food supply now, but what about six months from now? a year from now?"

"Before the summer has begun, Jeremiah, we won't be living down here. The rats are welcome to it then."

"We'll still be depending on it for food though. It's the only food left—unless you want to breed the rats. Personally, I've never liked the taste. And there's next winter to think about. With the little seed that's left for planting—even if it's still good—we can't possibly get through the winter. I don't like to live like this any more than the next man, but it's a way to survive. The only way, for the time being."

"Ah, that's a lot of hooey!" Neil said, in support of this father.

Anderson looked weary, and the lantern, which he had been holding up to examine the perforations of the wall of the passage, sank to his side. "You're right, Jeremiah. As usual." His lips curled in an angry smile, and he swung his bare foot (shoes were too precious to be wasted down here) at one of the ratholes from which two bright eyes had been staring up intently, examining the examiners. "Bastards!" he shouted. "Sons of bitches!" There was a squeal, and a fat, furry ball of ratflesh sailed on a high arc out of range of the lamplight. The whining, which had grown somewhat quieter, rose in volume, answering Anderson's challenge.

Orville put a hand on the old man's shoulder. His whole body was shaking with helpless rage. "Sir . . ." Orville protested. "Please."

"The bastard bit me," Anderson grumbled.

"We can't afford to scatter them now. Our best hope——"

"Half took off my toe," he said, stooping to feel the injury. "The bastard."

"—is to contain them here. To block up all the passages out of this tuber. Otherwise . . ." Orville shrugged. The alternative was clear.

"Then how do *we* get out?" Neil objected smugly.

"Oh, shut up, Neil," Anderson said wearily. "With what?" he asked Orville. "We haven't got anything a hungry rat couldn't chew his way through in five minutes."

"We have an axe though. We can weaken the walls of the roots so that they collapse in on themselves. The pressure at this depth is tremendous. That wood must be hard as iron, but if we can chip and scrape enough of it away at the right points, the earth itself will block the passages. Rats can't chew their way through basalt. There's a danger that the cave-in will get out of hand, but I think I can see that it won't. A mining engineer usually has to prevent cave-ins, but that's good training for someone who has to produce them."

"I'll let you try. Buddy, go back and get the axe—and anything else with a cutting edge. And send those other lotus-eaters up here. Neil and the rest of you, spread out to each of the entrances of this potato and do what you can to keep the rats inside. They don't seem very anxious to leave yet, but they may when the walls start tumbling down. Jeremiah, you come with me and show me what you mean to do. I don't understand why the whole thing isn't going to come down on our heads when we—God damn!"

"What is it?"

"My toe! Damned rat really took a hunk out of it. Well, we'll show these bastards!"

The extermination of the rats succeeded—if anything, too well. Orville attacked the first root at just the point where it belled outward to become the hard, spherical shell of the fruit. He worked hours, shaving off thin slices of wood, watching for any sign of stress that would give him an opportunity to escape, scraping away a little more, watching. When it came down, there was no warning. Suddenly Orville stood in the midst of thunder. He was lifted off his feet by the shock wave and hurled back into the passage.

The entire tuber had collapsed in upon itself.

Watchers at the other entrances reported no escaped rats, but there had been a fatality: one man, having missed his lunch (Anderson insisted that they eat only three times a day, and then sparingly), stepped into the tuber for a handful of fruit pulp at exactly the wrong moment. He, the fruit pulp and some few thousand rats were now being converted, at a modest, geological pace, into petroleum. A basalt wall of perfect, Euclidean flatness blocked each of the entrances to the tuber; it had come down quickly and neatly as a guillotine.

Anderson, who had not been present to witness the event (shortly after Orville had begun his work, he had had yet another fainting fit; they came more and more frequently of late), was incredulous when it was reported to him. Orville's *ex post facto* explanation did not convince him. "What's Buckminster What's-his-name got to do with anything? I ask a simple question, and you carry on about geographic domes."

"It's only a supposition. The walls of the tuber have to withstand incredible pressures. Buckminster Fuller was an architect—an engineer, if you prefer—who built things so they'd do just that. He designed skeletons, you might say. Designed them so that if the least part was weakened, the whole body would give way. Like when you remove the keystone of an arch—except that they were all keystones."

"This is a fine time to learn about Buckminster Fuller—when a man's been killed."

"I'm sorry, sir. I appreciate that it was my responsibility. I should have given more thought to the matter before rushing ahead."

"It can't be helped now. Go find Alice and bring her here. I'm coming down with a fever—and that ratbite hurts more every minute."

His responsibility indeed! Anderson thought, when Orville had left him. Well, it *would* be his responsibility soon enough. He had better call an assembly while he still had his wits about him and announce it for a fact.

But that would be tantamount to his own abdication. No, he would bide his time.

Meanwhile, he had had a new idea—a way of legitimizing Orville as his heir: Orville would become Anderson's son—his eldest son—by way of marriage.

But he balked at this step too. Blossom still seemed so young to him—hardly more than a child. Only a few months ago he had seen her with the other children playing jacks on the floor of the commonroom. Marriage? He would talk to Alice Nemerov about it. A woman always knew best about these things. Anderson and Alice were the two oldest survivors. That fact, and the death of Anderson's wife, had forced them willy-nilly into each other's confidence.

While he waited for her, he massaged his little toe. Where it had been bitten it was now numb; the pain was coming from the rest of the foot.

That night when the headcount was taken (Anderson being even less in a condition to do so), Orville and Buddy both came up with a figure of twenty-three. Neil, this time, counted twenty-four.

"He's slow," Buddy joked. "Give him time. He'll catch up with us yet."

Alice Nemerov, R.N., knew Anderson was going to die. Not just because she was a nurse and could recognize gangrene from its unremarkable inception. She had seen him begin to die long before he was bitten by the rat, even before the fainting fits had become a daily occurrence. When an old person is getting ready to die, you can see it all over him, written in neon. But because she *was* a nurse, and because she had come despite herself to like the old man, she tried to do something to keep him alive.

For this reason she had persuaded him to delay speaking to Orville and Blossom about his intentions for them. She led him on from day to day with a carrot of hope. At least it looked like hope.

At first, when the hope had been real, she had tried to suck off the infection, as in snakebite. The only effect was that she had grown nauseous and couldn't eat for two days. Now, half his foot was a dusky, dead blue. Decomposition would set in very quickly, if it had not already begun.

"Why don't you keep sucking off the infection?" Neil asked. He wanted to watch again.

"It wouldn't do any good now. He's dying."

"You could *try*. That's the least you could do." Neil bent down and examined his father's sleeping face. "Is he breathing better now?"

"Sometimes his breath comes very hard. Sometimes he scarcely seems to breathe at all. Neither symptom is out of the ordinary."

"His feet are cold," Neil said critically.

"What do you expect?" Alice snapped at him, past all patience. "Your father is dying. Don't you understand that? Only an amputation could save him at this point, and in his condition he couldn't survive amputation. He's worn out, an old man. He *wants* to die."

"That's not my fault, is it?" Neil shouted. Anderson woke for a moment at the noise, and Neil went away. His father had changed so much in the last few days that Neil felt awkward with him. It was like being with a stranger.

"The baby—is it a boy or a girl?" His voice was barely audible.

"We don't know yet, Mr. Anderson. It may take another hour. But no more than that. Everything is ready. She made the ligatures herself from scraps of rope. Buddy went up to the surface for a bucket of snow—he says it was a real March blizzard up there—and we've been able to sterilize the knife and wash out a couple of pieces of cotton. It won't be a hospital delivery, but I'm sure it will be all right."

"We must pray."

"*You* must pray, Mr. Anderson. You know I don't hold with those things."

Anderson smiled, and it was not, for a wonder, a really unpleasant expression. Dying seemed to mellow the old man; he had never been nicer than now. "You're just like my wife, just like Lady. She must be in hell for her sins and her scoffing, but hell can't be much worse than this. Somehow, though, I can't imagine her there."

"Judge not lest ye be judged, Mr. Anderson."

"Yes, Lady would always hark on that one too. It was her favorite Scripture."

Buddy interrupted them: "Time now, Alice."

"Go on, go on, don't dally here," Anderson urged. Unnecessarily, for she was already gone, taking the lamp with her. The darkness began to cover him like a woolen blanket, like a comforter.

If it's a boy, Anderson thought, *I can die happy.*

It was a boy.

Anderson was trying to say something. Neil could not make out quite what. He bent his ear closer to the old man's dry lips. He couldn't believe that his father was dying. His father! He didn't like to think about it.

The old man mumbled something. "Try and talk louder," Neil shouted into his good ear. Then to the others standing around: "Where's the lamp? Where's Alice? She should be here now. What are you all standing around like that for?"

"Alice is with the baby," Blossom whispered. "She said she'd be only another minute."

Then Anderson spoke again, loud enough for Neil but no one else to hear. "Buddy." That was all he said, though he said it several times.

"What'd he say?" Blossom asked.

"He said he wants to talk to me alone. The rest of you, go away and leave us together, huh? Dad's got things he wants to tell me alone."

There were shufflings and sighs as the few people who were not yet sleeping (the waking period having ended many hours ago) walked off into other areas of the tuber to leave father and son together. Neil strained to hear the least sound that would have meant that one of them remained nearby. In this abysmal darkness, privacy was never a sure thing.

"Buddy ain't here," he said at last, assured that they were alone. "He's with Maryann and the baby. So's Alice. There's some kind of problem about the way it breathes." Neil's throat was dry, and when he tried to make saliva and swallow it, it hurt. *Alice,* he thought angrily, *shouldn't be off somewhere else now.* All people talked about, it seemed to Neil, was the baby, the baby. He was sick of the baby. Did anybody care about *his* baby?

Curiously, Greta's lie had made its most lasting impression on Neil. He believed in it with the most literal, unquestioning faith, just as Maryann believed in Christ's virgin birth. Neil had the ability to brush

aside mere, inconvenient facts and considerations of logic like cobwebs. He had even decided that *his* baby's name was to be Neil Junior.
That would show old Buddy-boy!

"Then get Orville, will you?" Anderson whispered vexedly. "And
bring the others back. I have something to say."

"You can tell it to me, huh? Huh, Dad?"

"Get Orville, I said!" The old man began to cough.

"Okay, okay!" Neil walked some distance from the small hollow in
the fruit where his father was lying, counted to a hundred (skipping, in
his haste, everything between fifty-nine and seventy), and returned.
"Here he is, Dad, just like you said."

Anderson did not think it extraordinary that Orville should not greet
him. Everyone, these last days, was mute in his presence, the presence
of death. "I should have said this before, Jeremiah," he began, speaking
rapidly, afraid that this sudden renewal of strength would desert him
before he could finish. "I've waited too long. Though I know you've been
expecting it. I could tell by your eyes. So there was no need to——"
He broke off, coughing. "Here," (he gestured feebly in the darkness)
"take my revolver. There's only one bullet left, but some of them see it
as a sort of symbol. It's just as well to let them. There were so many
things I wanted to tell you, but there was no time."

Neil had grown more and more agitated during his father's valedic-
tory, and at last he could not contain himself: "What are you talking
about, Dad?"

Anderson chuckled. "He doesn't understand yet. Do *you* want to tell
him, or shall I?" There was a long silence. "Orville?" Anderson asked
in a changed voice.

"Tell me what, Dad? What don't I understand?"

"That Jeremiah Orville is taking over from now on. So bring him
here!"

"Dad, you don't mean that." Neil began to chew fretfully on his
lower lip. "He ain't an Anderson. He ain't even one of the village. Listen, Dad, I'll tell you what—I'll take over, huh? I'd do a better job than
him. Just give me a chance. That's all I ask, just one chance."

Anderson didn't reply. Neil began all over again, in a softer more
persuasive tone. "Dad you gotta understand—Orville ain't one of us."

"He will be soon enough, you little bastard. Now bring him here."

"What do you mean by that?"

"I mean I'm marrying him to your sister. Now cut out the crap and bring him here. And your sister too. Bring everybody here."

"Dad, you can't mean that, Dad!"

Anderson wouldn't say another word. Neil showed him all the reasons it was impossible for Orville to marry Blossom. Why, Blossom was only twelve years old! She was his sister—Neil's sister! Didn't he understand that? And who was this Orville character anyhow? He wasn't anybody. They should have killed him long ago, along with the other marauders. Hadn't Neil said so at the time? Neil would kill him now, if Anderson only said the word. How about it?

No matter what arguments Neil offered, the old man just lay there. *Was he dead?* Neil wondered. No, he was still breathing. Neil was in misery.

His keen ears picked up the sounds of others returning. "Leave us alone!" he shouted to them. They went away again, unable to hear Anderson's orders to the contrary.

"We've got to talk this thing over, you and me, Dad," Neil pleaded. Anderson wouldn't say a word, not a word.

With tears in his eyes, Neil did what he had to do. He pinched together the old man's nostrils and held his other hand down tightly over the old man's mouth. He wiggled around a little at first, but he was too weak to put up much of a struggle. When the old man was very, very quiet, Neil took his hands away and felt if he was still breathing.

He wasn't.

Then Neil took the holster and pistol off the old man and strapped it about his own thicker body. It was a sort of symbol.

Shortly afterward Alice came, with the lamp, and felt the dead man's wrist. "When did he die?" she asked.

"Just a minute ago." Neil said. It was hard to understand him, he was crying so. "And he asked me—he told me I should take his place. And he gave me his pistol."

Alice looked at Neil suspiciously. Then she bent over the face of the corpse and studied it attentively under the lamp. There were bruises on the sides of his nose, and his lip was cut and bleeding. Neil was bending over behind her. He couldn't understand where the blood had come from.

"You murdered him." Neil couldn't believe his ears: she hadn't called him *a murderer!*

He hit Alice over the top of the head with the butt of the pistol. Then he wiped away the blood trickling down his father's chin and spread fruit pulp over the cut lip.

More people came. He explained to them that his father was dead, that he, Neil Anderson, was to take over his father's place. He also explained that Alice Nemerov had let his father die when she could have saved him. All her talk about looking after the baby was so much hogwash. It was just as bad as if she had killed him outright. She would have to be executed, as an example. But not right away. For now they'd just tie her up. And gag her. Neil attended to the gag himself.

They obeyed him. They were accustomed to obeying Anderson, and they had been expecting Neil to take over from him for a long time— for years. Of course, they didn't believe Alice was in any way guilty, but then neither had they believed a lot of things Anderson had told them, and they'd always obeyed him anyhow. Maybe if Buddy had been there, he would have put up more of a fuss. But he was with Maryann and his newborn son, who was still weakly. They didn't dare bring the baby near his grandfather for fear of infection.

Besides, Neil was waving the Python around rather freely. They all knew there was a bullet left, and no one wanted to be the first to start an argument.

When Alice was securely bound, Neil asked where Orville was. Nobody, as it turned out, had seen or heard from him for several minutes.

"Find him and bring him here. Right now. Blossom! Where's Blossom? I saw her here a minute ago." But Blossom too was nowhere to be found.

"She's gotten lost!" Neil exclaimed, in a flash of understanding. "She's lost in the roots. We'll get up a search party. But first, find Orville. No—first help me with this." Neil grabbed up Alice by the shoulders. Somebody else took her feet. She didn't weigh more than a feedbag, and the nearest taproot where there was a sheer vertical drop wasn't two minutes away. They dropped her down the shaft. They couldn't see how far she fell, because Neil had forgotten to bring the lamp. No doubt, she fell a long, long way.

Now his father was revenged. Now he would look for Orville. There was only one bullet left in his father's Colt Python .357 Magnum. It was for Orville.

But *first* he must find Blossom. She must have run off somewhere when she heard her father was dead. Neil could understand that. The news had upset him too, upset him something terrible.

First, they'd look for Blossom. Then they'd look for Orville. He hoped, how he hoped, that he wouldn't find them together. That would be too awful for words.

TWELVE GHOSTS AND MONSTERS

You'd better hide, she thought, and that was how she got lost.

Once, when Blossom was seven, her parents had gone to Duluth for the weekend, taking the baby, Jimmie Lee, with them, leaving her alone in the big two-story house on the outskirts of Tassel. It was their eighteenth weeding anniversary. Buddy and Neil, both big boys then, had gone away—one to a dance, the other to a baseball game. For a while she had watched television, then she played with her dolls. The house became very dark, but it was her father's rule never to turn on more than one lamp at a time. Otherwise, you wasted current.

She didn't mind being a *little* scared. There was even something nice about it. So she turned off *all* the lights and pretended the Monster was trying to find her in the dark. Hardly daring to breathe and on the tips of her toes, she found safe hiding places for all her children: Lulu, because she was black anyway, in the coal bin in the basement; Ladybird, behind the cats' box; Nelly, the oldest, in the wastebasket by Daddy's desk. It got scarier and scarier. The Monster looked everywhere in the living room for her except the one place she was—behind the platform rocker. When he left the living room, Blossom crept up the stairs, keeping close to the wall so they wouldn't creak. But one *did* creak, and the Monster heard it and came gallumphing up the stairs behind her. With an excited shout she ran into the first room and shut the door behind her. It was Neil's bedroom, and the big horned moose-head glowered down at her from his place over the chest of drawers. She had always been afraid of that moose, but she was even more afraid of the Monster, who was out there in the hall, listening at every door to hear if she was inside.

She crept on hands and knees to Neil's closet door, which was ajar. She hid among the smelly old boots and dirty blue jeans. The door to the bedroom creaked open. It was so dark she couldn't see her hand in front of her face, but she could *hear* the Monster snuffling all over. He came to the door of the closet and stopped. He *smelled* she was inside. Blossom's heart almost stopped beating, and she prayed to God and to Jesus that the Monster would go away.

The Monster made a loud terrible noise and threw open the door, and for the very first time Blossom saw what the Monster looked like. She screamed and screamed and screamed.

Neil got home first that night, and he couldn't understand what Blossom was doing in his closet with his dirty blue jeans pulled down over her head, whimpering like she'd been whipped with the strap, and trembling like a robin caught in an April snowstorm. But when he picked her up, her little body became all rigid, and nothing would content her but that she sleep that night in Neil's bed. The next morning she'd come down with a fever, and her parents had to cut their trip short and come home and take care of her. No one ever understood what had happened, for Blossom didn't dare tell them about the Monster, whom *they* couldn't see. Eventually the incident was forgotten. As Blossom grew older, the content of her nightmares underwent a gradual change: the old monsters were no more terrifying now than the moosehead over the chest of drawers.

Darkness, however, is the very stuff of terror, and Blossom, running and creeping through the roots, descending depth after depth, felt the old fear repossess her. Suddenly all the lights in the house had been turned off. The darkness filled itself with monsters, like water pouring into a tub, and she ran down stairs and down hallways looking for a closet to hide in.

All through these last, long days of her father's dying, and even before, Blossom had been too much alone. She had felt that there was something he wanted to say to her but that he wouldn't let himself say it. This restraint humiliated her. She had thought that he did not want her to see him dying, and she had forced herself to stay away. Alice and Maryann, with whom she would customarily have passed her time, had no concern now but the baby. Blossom wanted to help them, but she was too young. She was at that age when one is uncomfortable in the presence of either birth or death. She haunted the fringes of these great events and pitied herself for being excluded from them. She imagined herself dying: how sad they would all be, how sorry they had neglected her!

Even Orville had no time for Blossom. He was either off by himself or at Anderson's side. Only Neil seemed more upset at the old man's death. Whenever Orville's path had crossed Blossom's he looked at her with such deadly intensity that the girl turned away, blushing and even slightly scared. No longer did she feel she understood him, and this, in a way, made her love him more—and more hopelessly.

But none of these things would have caused her to take flight, except into fantasies. It was only after she had seen the expression on Neil's face, the almost somnambulistic cast to his features, when she had heard him speak her name in that particular tone of voice—it was then that Blossom, like a doe catching scent of a hunter, panicked and began to run: away, into the deeper, sheltering dark.

She ran blindly, and so it was inevitable that she would go over one of the dropoffs into a primary root. It could happen, in the dark, even if you were careful. The void swallowed her whole.

Her bent knees first entered the pulp of the fruit, then her body pitched forward into the soft, yielding floss. She sank deep, deep into it. She landed unhurt, only a few inches away from the broken but still breathing body of Alice Nemerov, R.N.

He had delayed, had Jeremiah Orville, altogether too long. He had meant to revenge, and he had instead assisted. Day by day he had observed Anderson's death, his agony, his humiliation, and he knew that he, Jeremiah Orville, had had nothing to do with them. It was the Plant and mere happenstance that had brought Anderson low.

Orville had stood by, Hamletlike, and said *amen* to Anderson's prayers—had deceived only himself by his subtleties. He had been so greedy that all Anderson's sufferings proceed from himself alone and none from the Plant that he had led the old man and his tribe to a land of milk and honey. And now his enemy lay dying by the merest accident, by an infected bite on a vestigial toe.

Orville brooded, alone, in that deep darkness, and an image, a phantasm, took shape in the vacant air. Each day, the apparition took on greater definition, but he knew even from the first white shimmering that it was Jackie Whythe. But *this* was a Jackie who had never been: younger, lither, sweeter, the very essence of female grace and delicacy.

She made him, by all her familiar wiles, declare his love for her. He swore he loved her, but she was not satisfied, she would not believe him. She made him say it again and again.

She reminded him of the nights they had been together, of the treasures of her young body . . . and the horror of her death. Then she would ask again: *Do you love me?*

I do, I do, he insisted. *I do love you. Can you doubt it?* He was in an agony of desire to possess her once again. He craved a final kiss, the slightest touch, a breath merely, but he was refused.

I am dead, she reminded him, *and you have not revenged me.*

"Who will you have?" he asked aloud, grabbing up the axe, which he had been whetting on the palm of his hand all this while. "Give me the name, and with this same axe . . ."

Blossom, the phantasm whispered eagerly, not without a hint of jealousy. *You've abandoned me for that child. You court an infant.*

No! it was only that I might betray her. It was all for the sake of you.

Then betray her now. Betray her, and I will return to you. Then, only then, will I kiss you. Then, when you touch me, your hand will feel flesh. With those words she disappeared.

In the same instant he knew she had not been real, that this was, quite possibly, the inception of madness. But he did not care. Though she was not real, she was right.

Immediately he went in search of his victim. He found her standing on the edge of a group gathered about her father's corpse. Alice Nemerov was lying bound near the corpse, and Neil Anderson was there too, raving. Orville paid no heed to any of this. Then Blossom, as though sensing his purpose, ran madly into the dark tunnels of the Plant. He followed her. This time he would do what must be done—do it neatly, expeditiously, and with an axe.

Pressing the hard, crisp pulp from the rind of the fruit between her palms, Blossom was able to squeeze out a few oily drops of water. But it was so warm at this depth—eighty degrees or more—that she could hardly hope to revive Alice with it. She began again to massage the old woman's thin hands, her cheeks, the sagging flesh of her arms. Mechanically she repeated the same few words of comfort: "Alice dear, please. . . . *Try* to wake up, try. . . . Alice, it's *Blossom*. . . . Alice? . . . It's all right now. . . . Oh, *please!*" At last the old woman seemed to be conscious, for she groaned.

"Are you all right? Alice?"

Alice made a noise verging on speech, which was terminated by a hissing intake of breath. When she did speak, when she could speak, her voice was unnaturally loud and strangely resolute. "My hip. I think . . . yes, it's broken."

"Oh no! Oh, Alice! Does it . . . does it hurt?"

"Like hell, my dear."

"Why did he do it? Why did Neil—" Blossom paused; she dared not say what it was that Neil had done. Now that Alice was conscious, her own fear and agitation settled over her again. It was as though she had revived Alice only that she might be able to tell her, Blossom, that the Monster wasn't real, just something she'd imagined.

"Why did he throw me down here? Because, my dear, the bastard murdered your father, and because I knew it and was fool enough to say so. And then, I fancy, he never *has* liked me very much."

Blossom said she would not believe it, that it was absurd. She made Alice tell her how she knew, called for the evidences, refuted them. She made her, suffering as she was, repeat each detail of the story, and still she would not believe it. Her brother had faults, but he was not a murderer.

"He murdered *me,* didn't he?" It was a difficult question to answer.

"Buy *why* would he do such a thing? Why kill a man who's almost dead? It makes no sense. There was no reason."

"It was on your account, my dear."

Blossom could almost feel the Monster breathing down her neck. "What do you mean?" She grabbed Alice's hand almost angrily. "Why on *my* account?"

"Because he must have found out that your father was intending for you and Jeremiah Orville to be married."

"Daddy intended—I don't understand?"

"He wanted Jeremiah to be the new leader, to take his place. He didn't *want* it, but he saw that it would have to be that way. But he put off telling anyone about it. That was my doing. I told him to wait. I thought it would keep him going. I never thought . . ."

Alice talked on, but Blossom had stopped listening. She understood now what her father had wanted to tell her and why he had hesitated. Grief and shame flooded over her: she had misjudged him; she had left him all those days to suffer alone. And he had only wanted her happiness, the happiness she wanted for herself! If only she could return to beg his forgiveness, to thank him. It was as though Alice, by those few words, had turned on all the lights in the house and restored her father to life.

But Alice's next words dispelled this illusion. "You'd better watch out for him," she said grimly. "You dare not trust him. *Especially* you."

"Oh no, no, you don't understand. I love him. And I think he loves me too."

"Not Orville. Of course he loves you. Any fool can see that. It's Neil you'd better watch out for. He's crazy."

Blossom did not protest this. She knew, better than Alice, though less aware till now, how true this was.

"And part of his craziness has to do with you."

"When the others know what he's done, when I tell them . . ." Blossom did not have to say more than this. When the others knew what Neil had done, he would be killed.

"That's why I told you. So they *would* find out."

"You'll tell them yourself. We've got to get back. *Now.* Here—put your arm around my shoulder." Alice protested, but Blossom would not listen. The old woman was light. Blossom could carry her, if need be.

An agonized cry parted the old woman's lips, and she tore her arm away from Blossom. "No! no, the pain. . . . I can't."

"Then I'll get help."

"What help? Whose help? A doctor? An ambulance? I couldn't help your father recover from a rat bite, and this is——" The sound that intruded upon her speech was more eloquent than any words she might have intended.

For a long while, Blossom bit her lip to keep silent. When she felt Alice was ready to listen, she said, "Then I'll just sit here with you."

"And watch me die? It will take a while. No more than two days, though, and most of the time I'll be making these awful noises. No— that would be no comfort to me. But there is something you can do. If you're strong enough."

"Whatever it is, I'll do it."

"You must promise." Blossom's hand tightened over hers in assurance. "You must do for me what Neil did for your father."

"*Murder* you? No! Alice, you can't ask me to——"

"My dear, I've done it in my time for those who have asked. Some of them had less reason than I. A hypodermic of air, and the pain is—" She did not, this time, cry out. "—gone. Blossom, I *beg* you."

"Someone may come. We'll make a stretcher."

"Yes, someone may come. Neil may come. Can you imagine what he would do if he finds me still alive?"

"No, he wouldn't——" But immediately she knew he would.

"You *must*, my dear. I'll hold you to your promise. But kiss me first. No, not like that—on the lips."

Blossom's trembling lips pressed against Alice's that were rigid with the effort to hold back the pain. "I love you," she whispered. "I love you like my very own mother."

Then she did what Neil had done. Alice's body twisted away in instinctive, unthinking protest, and Blossom let loose her grip.

"No!" Alice gasped. "Don't torture me—do it!"

Blossom did not let loose this time until the old woman was dead.

The darkness grew darker, and Blossom thought she could hear someone climbing down the vines of the root overhead. There was a loud terrible noise as his body came down into the fruit pulp. Blossom knew what the Monster would look like: he would look like Neil. She screamed and screamed and screamed.

The Monster had an axe.

"Return soon," she begged.

"I will, I promise." Buddy bent down to his wife, missing her lips in the darkness (the lamp, by Neil's authority, was to remain with the corpse) and kissing her nose instead. She giggled girlishly. Then, with an excess of caution, he touched one finger to the tiny arm of his son. "I love you," he said, not bothering to define whether he was addressing her or the infant or perhaps both. He did not know himself. He only knew that despite the terrible events of the last months, and especially of the past hour, his life seemed meaningful in a way that it had not for years. The somberest considerations could not diminish the fullness of his hopes nor dampen the glow of his satisfaction.

In even the worst disaster, in the largest defeats, the machinery of joy keeps on grinding for a lucky few.

Maryann seemed more aware than he that their charmed circle was of very small circumference, for she murmured, "Such a terrible thing."

"What?" Buddy asked. His attention was taken up with Buddy Junior's teeny-tiny toe.

"Alice. I can't understand why he———"

"He's crazy," Buddy said, moving reluctantly outside the circle. "Maybe she called him a name. She has—she *had* a sharp tongue, you know. When he gets back, I'll see that something's done. There's no telling what rotten thing he'll do next. Orville will help, and there are others, too, who've let a word drop. But in the meantime he has a gun and we don't. And the important thing now is to find Blossom."

"Of course. That must come first. It's just that it's such a terrible thing."

"It's a terrible thing," he agreed. He could hear Neil calling to him again. "I have to go now." He began to move away.

"I wish the lamp were here, so I could see you one more time."

"You sound like you don't think I'll return."

"No! Don't say that—even as a joke. You *will* come back. I know you will. But, Buddy———?"

"Maryann?"

"Say it one more time."

"I love you."

"And I love you." When she was quite sure he was gone, she added: "I've *always* loved you."

The several members of the descending search party threaded their way through the labyrinth of divergent roots on a single slim rope, braided by Maryann from the fiber of the vines. When any member of the party separated from the main body, he attached the end of his own reel of rope to the communal rope that led back to the tuber where Anderson was lying in state beside the vigilant lamp.

Neil and Buddy descended the farthest along the communal rope. When it gave out, they were at a new intersection of roots. Buddy knotted one end of his rope to the end of the main line and went off to the left. Neil, having done likewise, went to the right, but only for a short distance. Then he sat down and thought, as hard as he could think.

Neil did not trust Buddy. Never had. Now, with their father passed on, wouldn't he have to trust him still less? He thought he was so smart, Buddy did, with that brat of his. Like he was the only man in the world ever had a son. Neil hated his guts for other reasons too—which his mind shied from. It would not do for him to be too consciously aware that the presumable Neil Junior, if he existed at all, existed most probably as a result of other seed than his own. That was a thought that he had best not think at all.

Neil was worried. He sensed in several of the men who'd gone out on the search a resistance to his authority, and this resistance seemed strongest in Buddy. A leader can't afford to let his leadership be challenged. Their father had always harped on that. It didn't seem to make any difference to Buddy that Anderson had *wanted* Neil to take over for him. Buddy had always been a wild one, a rebel, an atheist.

That's what he is! Neil thought, astonished at how perfectly the word defined everything dangerous in his brother. *An atheist!* Why hadn't he realized that before?

One way or another, atheists had to be stomped out. Because atheism was like poison in the town reservoir; it was like . . . But Neil couldn't remember how the rest of it went. It had been a long time since his father had given a good sermon against atheism and the Supreme Court.

On the heels of this perception another new idea came to Neil. It was, for him, a true inspiration, a revelation—almost as though his father's spirit had come down from heaven and whispered it in his ear.

He would tie Buddy's line in a circle!

Then, when Buddy tried to get back, he'd just keep following the rope around and around the circle. Once you grasped the basic concept, it was a very simple idea.

There was one hitch, however, when you thought about it carefully. One part of the circle would be here at this intersection, and Buddy could feel around, maybe, and discover the end of the main line where it was still knotted to Neil's.

But he wouldn't if the circle didn't touch this intersection!

Chuckling to himself, Neil unknotted Buddy's rope and began following Buddy, winding the rope up as he went along. When he figured he'd taken up enough of it, he turned off along a minor branch of the root, unwinding the rope as he crawled along. This small root connected to another equally small, and this to yet another. The roots of the Plant were always circling around on themselves, and if you just kept turning the same direction, you usually came back to the point you started from. And sure enough, Neil soon was back in the larger root, where he caught hold of Buddy's line, stretched taut, a foot off the floor. Buddy was probably not far away.

Neil's trick was working splendidly. Having nearly reached the end of the length of rope, he knotted it to the other end and formed a perfect circle.

Now, Neil thought, with satisfaction, *let him try and find his way back. Let him try and make trouble now! The lousy atheist!*

Neil began to crawl back the way he had come, using Buddy's rope as a guide, laughing all the way. Only then did he notice that there was some kind of funny slime all over his hands and all over his clothing too.

THIRTEEN CUCKOO, JUG-JUG, PU-WE, TO-WITTA-WO!

There are people who cannot scream even when the occasion calls emphatically for screaming. Any drill sergeant can tell you of men, good soldiers every other way, who, when they must run forward to plant a bayonet in the guts of a sawdust dummy, cannot let loose with any sort of battle cry—or at best can manage some bloodless imitation, a half-hearted *Kill Kill Kill!* It is not that these men lack the primordial emotions of hatred and bloodlust; they have just become too civilized, too bound in, to experience a pure berserker rage. Perhaps a real battle will bring it out of them; perhaps nothing will.

There are emotions more primordial, more basic to survival, than hatred and bloodlust; but it is the same with them too—they can be stifled, covered over with civilized form and secondary modes of feeling. Only extreme circumstances can release them.

Jeremiah Orville was a very civilized man. The last seven years had liberated him in many ways, but they had not effaced his civilization until very lately, when events had taught him to desire the consummation of his revenge above his own happiness and safety. It was a beginning.

But as he stood beside Blossom, the axe in his hand unseen, himself unseen, hearing these heartrending cries that fear wrenched from her throat, now the more primordial emotion of love overcame him, shattered the civilized Jeremiah, and, dropping the weapon, he fell to his knees and began kissing the young body that was now the most important and beautiful thing in the world.

"Blossom!" he cried with joy. "O Blossom! Blossom!" and continued senselessly to repeat her name.

"Jeremiah! You! My God, I thought it was *him*!"

And he, in the same instance: "How could I have loved *her*, a ghost, bodiless, when all this while—— Forgive me! Can you forgive me?"

She could not understand him. "*Forgive* you!" She laughed and cried, and they said many things to each other then without thinking, without caring to understand any more than the as-yet-unassimilable fact that they were in love.

Passion's highest flights tend to be, if not completely innocent, slow. Orville and Blossom could not enjoy the happiness of gazing hours-long into each other's eyes, but the darkness permitted as much as it denied. They dallied; they delayed. They called each other by the simple, affectionate names of schoolgirl romances (names that had never passed between Orville and Jackie Whythe, who had been given, when Orville's hands moved over her, to cruder expressions—a certain sign of sophistication), and these *sweethearts,* these *darlings* and *my very owns,* seemed to express philosophies of love exact as arithmetic and subtle as music.

Eventually, as they must, a few words of common sense disturbed the perfect solitude of their love, like pebbles thrown in a still pond. "The others must be looking for me," she said. "I have to tell them about something."

"Yes I know—— I was listening up above as Alice spoke to you."

"Then you know that Daddy wanted this. He was going to say so when——"

"Yes, I know."

"And Neil——"

"I know that too. But you needn't worry about him now." He kissed the soft, drooping lobe of her ear. "Let's not speak of it though. Later, we'll do what we have to do."

She pushed Orville away from her. "No, Jeremiah. Listen—let's go away somewhere. Away from them and all their hating and jealousy. Somewhere where they'll never find us. We can be like Adam and Eve and think of new names for all the animals. There's the whole world——" She did not say any more, for she realized that there *was* the whole world. She stretched out a hand to draw Orville back to her—and to push the world aside for a little longer—but instead of Orville's living flesh her hand encountered Alice's fractured hip.

A voice, not Orville's, called her name. "Not *yet,*" she whispered. "It can't end *now.*"

"It won't end," he promised, helping her to her feet. "We have our whole life ahead of us. A lifetime lasts forever. At my age, I should know."

She laughed. Then, for the whole world to hear, she shouted: "We're down here. Go away, whoever you are. We'll find our way back by ourselves."

But Buddy had already found them, entering the tuber by a side passage. "Who's that with you?" he asked. "Orville, is it you? I should knock your block off for pulling a stunt like this. Don't you know the old man is dead? What a hell of a time to elope!"

"No, Buddy, you don't understand. It's all right—Orville and I are in love."

"Yeah, I understand that all right. He and I'll have a talk about that—in private. I only hope I got here before he could put your *love* to the test. For Christ's sake, Orville—this girl is only fourteen! She's young enough to be your daughter. The way you're going at it, she's young enough to be your *grand*daughter."

"Buddy! It's not like that at all," Blossom protested. "It's what father *wanted* for us. He said to Alice and then——"

Buddy, moving forward with their voices as a guide, stumbled over the nurse's dead body. "What in hell!"

"That's Alice. If you'd only *listen*——" Blossom broke into tears in which frustration mingled with sorrow.

"Sit down," Orville said, "and shut up for a minute. You've been jumping to the wrong conclusions, and there are a lot of things you don't know. No—don't argue, man, *listen!*

"The question, then, is not what should be done in Neil's case, but who's to do it," Orville concluded. "I don't think I should have to bear that responsibility, nor that you should either. Personally, I've never liked your father's high-handed way of being judge, jury, and law all by himself. It's an honor to have been nominated as his successor, but an honor I'd rather decline. This is a matter for the community to act on."

"Agreed. I know that if *I* did . . . what has to be done, they'd say it was for personal reasons. and it just wouldn't be true. I don't want anything he's got. Not any more. In fact, the only thing I want right now is to go back and see Maryann and my son again."

"Then the thing to do is to set about finding the others. Blossom and I can stay out of the way until the matter has been settled. Neil can be king for a day, but he'll have to sleep sometime, and that will be time enough to depose him."

"Fine. We'll go now—but not back along my rope. It would be too easy to run into Neil that way. If we climb up the vines of the root that you came down, there'll be no danger of our crossing his path."

"If Blossom's up to it, I'm agreeable."

"Jeremiah, you strange old man, I can climb up those things twice as fast as any thirty-five-year-old, two-hundred pound grandfather."

Buddy heard what he supposed was a kiss and pursed his lips in disapproval. Though he agreed in theory with all that Orville had said in his own and Blossom's defense—that times had changed, that early marriage was now positively to be preferred to the old way, that Orville (this had been Blossom's argument) was certainly the most eligible of the survivors, and that they had Anderson's posthumous blessing on their union—despite all these cogent reasons, Buddy could not help feeling a certain distaste for the whole thing. *She's still a child,* he told himself, and against this, to him, incontrovertible fact all their reasonings seemed as specious as the proofs that Achilles can never pass the tortoise in their endless footrace.

But he swallowed his distaste, as a child swallows some loathed vegetable in order to go outside and do something more important. "Let's shove off," he said.

To return to the primary root down which Blossom and Orville had dropped it was necessary to detour back along the way Buddy had come and then angle up along a branch root so narrow that even crawling through it was arduous.

But this was only a foretaste of the difficulties they faced in climbing the vertical root. The vines by which they hoped to ascend were covered over with a thin film of slime; the hand could not grip them firmly enough to keep from slipping. Only at the nodal points, where the vines fed into each other, forming a sort of stirrup (like the system of roots, these vines were forever joining and rejoining), could one purchase a secure hold, and there was not always certain to be another such nodal intersection of vines within grasping distance overhead. They had continually to backtrack and reascend along a different network of vines. Even more frustrating was that their feet (though bare, they were not prehensile) were constantly slipping out of these makeshift stirrups. It was like trying to climb a greased rope ladder with rungs missing.

"What's to be gained killing ourselves?" Buddy asked rhetorically, after having come within one slippery fingerhold of doing exactly this for himself. "I don't know where this slop is coming from, but it doesn't seem to be letting up. The higher we go, the more likely we are to break our necks if we fall. Why not go back along my rope after all? It's not that likely we'll run into Neil, and if we do, we don't have to let on that we know anything he wouldn't want us to. I'd rather risk five, ten minutes with him than another hundred yards up this greased chimney."

This seemed a sensible course, and they returned to the tuber. The descent was easy as sliding down a firepole.

Following Buddy's line up a mild slope, they noticed that here too the vines were slimed and slippery beneath their bare feet. Feeling down beneath the layer of vines, Orville discovered that a little rivulet of the slime was flowing down the slope.

"What is it, do you suppose?" Buddy wondered.

"I think the springtime has come at last," Orville replied.

"And this is the sap—of course! I recognize the feel of it now—and the smell—oh, don't I know that smell!"

"Springtime!" Blossom said. "We'll be able to return to the surface!"

Happiness is contagious (and wasn't there every reason for a young man newly in love to be happy in any case?), and Orville quoted part of a poem he remembered:

"Spring, the sweet Spring, is the year's pleasant king;
Then blooms each thing, then maids dance in a ring,
Cold doth not sting, the pretty birds do sing,
Cuckoo, jug-jug, pu-we, to-witta-wo!"

"What a lovely poem!" she said, catching hold of his hand and squeezing.

"What a lot of nonsense!" Buddy said. *"Cuckoo, jug-jug, pu-we, to-witta-wo!"*

The three of them laughed gaily. The sun seemed to be shining on them already, and nothing was needed to make them laugh again but that one of them repeat the silly old Elizabethan words.

Some two thousand feet above their heads, the reviving land basked under the bright influence of the sun, which had indeed passed the equinox. Even before the last patches of snow had melted from the southern sides of boulders, the leaves of the great Plants unfurled to receive the light and began without further ado to set about their work as though October were only yesterday.

Except for the noise of the leaves snapping open (and that was over in a day), it was a silent spring. There were no birds to sing.

The leaves spoke hungrily to the stems, drained dry to last out the freezing northern winter, and the stems spoke to the roots, where the solute-bearing sap, which the leaves needed to make new food, began to boil up through myriad capillaries. Where these capillaries had been broken by the passage of man, the sap oozed forth and spread over the vines that lined the hollows of the roots. As more and more sap poured through the arteries of the awakening Plant, the thin sap formed little rivulets, which, merging with other rivulets, became little streams, and these streams ran down to flood the lowest depths of the roots. When they flowed into hollows in which the capillaries were still intact, they were reabsorbed, but elsewhere the levels of these streams rose higher and higher, flooding the roots, like sewers in a sudden March thaw.

Now the tubers of the fruit, which had been forming for years, took on a fine, autumnal richness. The airy floss at their cores, receiving their final supplies of food from the leaves above, thickened to the consistency of whipped egg white.

In both hemispheres, the Plant was coming to the end of a long season, and now, at regular intervals over the green earth, there descended from the spring skies gleaming spheres so immense that each one, landing, crushed several of the Plants under its ponderous bulk. Viewed from the proper distance, the landscape would have resembled a bed of clover overspread with gray basketballs.

These gray basketballs basked a few hours in the sun, then extruded, from apertures at their bases, hundreds of exploratory cilia, each of which moved toward a nearby Plant and with tidy, effective little drill bits, began to bore down through the woody stem into the hollow of the root below. When a satisfactory passage had been opened, the cilium was drawn back into the gray basketball.

The harvest was being prepared.

Neil had gone three times about the circle of rope he had fashioned to trap Buddy, and he was beginning, dully, to sense that he had been caught in his own snare (though *how* it had happened he did not yet understand). Then, as he had feared, Buddy could be heard returning along the root. Blossom and Orville were with him, all of them laughing! At him? He had to hide, but there was nowhere to hide, and he didn't want to hide from Blossom anyhow. So he said, "Uh, hi." They stopped laughing.

"What are you doing *here*?" Buddy asked.

"Well, you see, uh . . . This rope here, it keeps . . . No, that's not it, either." The more he talked the more confused he became, and the more impatient Buddy.

"Oh, never mind then. Come along. I've found Blossom. And Orville too. Let's round up the others now. It's spring. Haven't you noticed the slime—Hey—what's this?" He had found the point where the end of his own rope was knotted to its own middle. "This surely isn't the intersection where we left each other. I'd remember if I'd gone down any root as small as this."

Neil didn't know what to do. He wanted to hit his snoopy brother over the head, that's what he *wanted* to do, and shoot Orville, just blast his brains out. But he sensed that this had better be done away from Blossom, who might not understand. Then too, when you're lost the most important thing is to get home safe. When you're home safe, things won't seem so muddled as when you're lost.

A whispered conversation was going on among Buddy, Orville and Blossom. Then Buddy said: "Neil, did you——"

"No! I don't know how . . . it just must of *happened*! It's not *my* fault!"

"Well, you dumb clod!" Buddy began to laugh. "Why, if you had to saw a limb off a tree, I swear you'd sit on the wrong side to do it. You've tied my line in a circle, haven't you?"

"No, Buddy, honest to God! Like I said, I don't know how——"

"And you didn't bring your own line along so you could get back. Oh, Neil, how do you do it? How do you always find a way?"

Orville and Blossom joined Buddy's laughter. "Oh, *Neil*!" Blossom cried out. "Oh, *Neil*!"

That made Neil feel good, to hear Blossom say his name like that, and he began to laugh along with everybody else. The joke was on him!

Surprisingly, it seemed that Buddy and Orville weren't going to make a big stink. Maybe they knew what was good for them!

"It seems we'll have to find our way back as best we can," Orville said with a sigh, when they were all done laughing. "Neil, would you like to lead the way?"

"No," Neil said, somber again and touching the Python in his holster for assurance. "No, I'll be the leader, but I'll bring up the rear."

An hour later they had come up against a dead end, and they knew they were thoroughly lost. It was no longer possible to shatter the capillaries with a wave of one's arm. They were swollen with sap and resilient. It would have been no more difficult to crawl through a honeycomb than through the unopened hollows. They were compelled therefore to stay strictly within the bounds of paths already blazed. Thanks to Anderson's explorations, there were quite enough of these. Quite too many.

Orville summed up their situation. "It's back to the sub-basement, my dears. We'll have to take another elevator to get to the ground floor."

"What'd you say?" Neil asked.

"I said——"

"I heard what you said! And I don't want you to use that word again, understand? You remember who's leader here, huh?"

"What word, Neil?" Blossom asked.

"My dears!" Neil screamed. Neil had always been able to scream when he felt the occasion called for it. He was not overcivilized, and the

primordial was very close to the surface of his mind. It seemed to grow closer all the time.

FOURTEEN **THE WAY UP**

The quiet, which for months had been absolute, was broken by the trickling of the sap. It was a sound like the sound of water in early spring, flowing through the town gutters underneath unmelted banks of snow.

While they rested they did not speak, for the most innocuous statements could throw Neil into a state of hysterical excitement. Naturally, they knew better than mention Anderson or Alice, but why, when Buddy began to worry out loud about his wife and son, should Neil complain that he was "selfish," that all he thought about was sex? When Orville spoke of their predicament and speculated (with more good cheer than he felt) on their chances of reaching the surface, Neil thought they were blaming him. Silence seemed altogether the best policy, but Neil could not endure more than a few moments of silence either. Then he would start to complain: "If only we'd brought down the lamp, we wouldn't be having any trouble now." Or, remembering one of his father's favorite themes: "Why do I have to do the thinking for everybody? Why is that?"

Or he would whistle. His favorite tunes were the *Beer-Barrel Polka, Red River Valley, Donkey Serenade* (which he accompanied persuasively with the popping of his cheeks) and the theme from *Exodus.* Once he had started any of these, he could go on *perpetuum mobile* for the duration of the time they rested. It wouldn't have been so bad if he'd been able to stay in the same key for eight bars running.

It was hardest for Buddy. Blossom and Orville had each other. In the darkness they would hold each other's hands, while Neil ground out the tune one more time around, like a diligent monkey; they could even kiss, quietly.

———

Here there was neither north nor south, east nor west; there was only up and down. There were no measurable units of distance, only rough estimates of temperature and depth, and their only measure of elapsed time was the time it took their bodies to drop, too exhausted to continue without another rest.

They never knew whether they were at the periphery or near the heart of the labyrinth. They might ascend, through channels already opened, to within a few hundred feet—or even ten—of the surface only to find themselves at a dead end. It was necessary not simply to find a way up but to find *the* way up. It was hard to make Neil understand why this was so. When Blossom had explained it to him, he had seemed to agree, but later when Orville brought up the subject again, the argument started all over.

They were soaked through with their own sweat and with the sap, which in the least steep roots reached levels of four and five inches. After hours of climbing they were at a height where the heat was not so overwhelming (the lower depths felt like a sauna), and the air seemed to be gas again. Orville estimated the temperature as seventy-five, which placed them a probable fifteen hundred feet from the surface. Ordinarily, over a known route, they could have climbed that height in little more than three hours. Now it might very well take days.

Orville had hoped that the flow of sap would abate as they reached higher levels; instead it was worsening. Where did it all come from? The logistics of the Plant's water supply was something he had never stopped to consider. Well, he couldn't stop now either.

You couldn't just grab hold of a vine and haul yourself up the slope; you had to make your hand into a sort of hook and slip it into a stirrup. You couldn't just reach back and help the next person up after you; you had to grapple the two hooks together. So it was always the hands that hurt worst and were first to give out. You'd hang there and feel them letting loose, and you'd hope that you wouldn't slide back with the sap too far. Once you let go, it wasn't so bad—you'd slide along soft and easy if the slope wasn't too steep, or else shoot down like a toboggan, until you came up against someone or something with a bump, and then you had to get your hooks bent back into shape and start clawing your way back up through the slime. But you knew your body could go a long way yet, and you hoped that would be far enough.

They might have been climbing twelve or twice twelve hours. They had eaten and rested a few times, but they had not slept. They had not slept, in fact, since before the night of Anderson's dying and Maryann's delivery. Now it must be night again. Their minds were leaden with the necessity for sleep.

"Absolute necessity," Orville repeated.

Neil objected. This was just going to be a resting period. He feared that if he went to sleep first, they would take away his gun. They weren't to be trusted. But if he just sat here and let his body *relax* . . . dog-tired, that's what he . . .

He was the first to sleep after all, and they didn't take his gun. They didn't care. They didn't want his gun: they only wanted to sleep.

Neil's repertoire of dreams was no larger than his stock of songs. First he dreamed his baseball dream. Then he was walking up the stairs of the old house in town. Then he dreamed of Blossom. Then he dreamed his baseball dream again, except this time it was different: when he opened the closet door, his father was the first baseman. Blood spurted from the deep cleft of the first baseman's mitt, which opened and closed, opened and closed, in the dead man's hand. But otherwise the dreams were just the same as always.

The next day, after an hour or so, the hurt went out of their hands, and it was the stickiness that was hardest to endure. Their clothes clung to their straining limbs or hung loose and heavy like skins that could not be sloughed off. "We'd move faster," Orville said, "if we weren't weighted down with these denim jackets."

Somewhat later, since it appeared that the idea was not going to come to Neil of itself, Buddy added, "If we knotted our jackets together, sleeve to sleeve, and used them for rope, we could climb faster."

"Yeah," Neil said, "but you're forgetting there's a lady with us."

"Oh, don't bother about *me*," Blossom protested.

"Just our jackets, Neil. It wouldn't be any different than going swimming."

"No!" The strident tone was creeping into his voice again. "It wouldn't be *right*!" There was no use arguing with him once he had made up his mind. He was their leader.

The next time they stopped to rest and eat, the sap was raining down on them in great globs, like the water drops that announce a summer thunderstorm. The central stream of sap flowing through the root was now well over their ankles. As soon as they were not quite sopping wet, their clothes stuck to them like suits of adhesive tape. They could move freely only when they were drenched.

"I can't stand it any longer," Blossom said, beginning to cry. "I can't *stand* it."

"There now, Miss Anderson. Chin up! Tally-ho! Remember the Titanic!"

"Stand what?" Neil asked.

"These clothes," she said. And indeed that was a part of what she couldn't stand.

"Oh, I guess she's right," Neil said, as uncomfortable as the others. "It can't hurt if we just take off our jackets. Hand them to me, and I'll knot the sleeves together."

"Good idea!" Orville said. They all handed their jackets to Neil.

"Blossom!" he said. "I didn't mean *you*. It isn't right." She didn't say anything. Neil sort of giggled. "Well, if that's the way you want it," he said.

The stuff gushed from the small opening above as from a burst water main. Quite properly, it could not be called sap. It was more like water. For a while they were happy because it cleaned them off. But it was cold, too cold.

The roots, as they ascended through them, had been growing smaller instead of larger. To get through them now they had to crawl on hands and knees, and even so they could scrape their heads on the ceiling if they weren't careful. The water was up to their elbows.

"I think," Orville said cautiously, "that we're coming up underneath

Lake Superior. This much water can't be coming from spring thaws." He waited for Neil to protest. Then, still more cautiously: "I think we'll have to go back the way we came. Let's hope we have better luck a second time."

The reason Neil had not protested was that he had not heard. Orville's voice had been drowned out by the roar of the water, which acres and acres of thirsty Plants were siphoning from the lake bottom. Orville explained his theory several times over when they had backed off to a quieter spot. Then Blossom tried.

"Neil, look, it's very simple—the only way away from the lake is *down*. Because if we try to move along at *this* level, we can as easily be going east—farther on into the lake—as west—away from it. If we had the lamp, we could use your compass, but we don't have the lamp. We might just go along north or south and follow the shore. There's no telling how much area beneath the lake Daddy explored last winter. We just have to go *down*. Do you understand?"

Orville took advantage of this occasion to have some private words with Buddy: "What the hell—let's leave him here if he doesn't want to go with us. It'll be his own fault if he drowns."

"No," said Buddy, "that wouldn't be *right*. I want to do this by the book."

"Okay, I'll go," Neil told Blossom, "but I think it's a lot of hooey. I'm only agreeing for your sake. Remember that."

Down: the sap was in spate. It jostled their bodies together or tore them apart as casually as floodwaters bearing off the trees of the riverbank. Strong currents dashed them against the walls of the root wherever the curves were too sharp or too steep. Days of climbing were retraced in minutes.

Deeper down: the stream became less chill, grew thicker, like pudding coming to a boil. But its pace did not slacken. It was like going down a ski trail on a piece of cardboard. At least they need not worry about repeating their mistake: it was no longer possible to move "upstream" toward the lake.

At this depth there were now whole stretches where the hot sap filled the entire hollow of the root. Hoarding a lungful of air, Orville (who was the first to test any new passage) followed the current resistlessly and hoped. There had always been some branch root feeding into the flooded root from above, too small to ascend through perhaps but large enough to butt one's head into for a breath of air. But the next time, of course, there might not be such an opening. There might only be a dead end.

That fear—that the current was leading them down a blind alley— absorbed their whole attention. More and more often their bodies were swept into entangling networks of the sap-swollen capillaries that lined the unexplored passages. Once Orville was caught in such a net where the root had split abruptly in two. Buddy and Blossom, next behind, found him there, his legs moving only as the current moved them. His head had struck against the hard wedge separating the two branches of the root. He was unconscious, perhaps drowned.

They hauled at his pants leg, and his pants slid right off his narrow hips. Then they each took a foot and pulled him out. A short distance away they found an area where the root, sloping gently upward, was only half-filled with sap. Buddy embraced Orville in a bear hug and began squeezing the water out of his lungs, rhythmically. Then Blossom tried mouth-to-mouth respiration, which she'd learned in Red Cross swimming classes.

"What are you doing?" Neil asked. Unfamiliar sounds made him nervous.

"She's giving Orville artificial respiration," Buddy answered testily. "He half-drowned back there."

Neil reached out fingers to confirm this. The fingers came between Orville's mouth and Blossom's, then clamped down tightly over Orville's. "You're *kissing* him!"

"Neil!" Blossom screamed. She tried to tear away her brother's fingers, but even desperation did not lend her sufficient strength. One can only be desperate so long, and she'd passed that limit long ago. "You'll kill him!"

Buddy struck a blow in the direction he supposed Neil to be, but it glanced off Orville's shoulder. Neil began to drag Orville's body away.

"He doesn't have pants on either," Neil fretted.

"They came off when we were pulling him out. We told you that, remember?"

The sudden deprivation of oxygen, coming after their efforts at revival, proved to be exactly the stimulus Orville required—he came to.

When the body he was carrying began to stir, Neil let go abruptly, spooked. He had thought Orville was dead, or very nearly.

Buddy and Neil than had a long debate on the propriety of nudity (both in the particular case of Orville and in general) under the present, exceptional circumstances. The argument was mainly a pretext on Buddy's part to give Orville a chance to regain his strength. "Do you want to get back to the surface," Buddy asked, "or do you want to stay down here and be drowned?"

"No!" Neil said, yet once more. "It isn't right. *No!*"

"You've got to *choose*. Which is it?" Buddy was pleased to discover that he could play on Neil's fears as easily as on a harmonica. "Because if we're going to go *up,* we'll have to go up together, and we'll need some kind of rope."

"We *had* a rope."

"And you lost it, Neil."

"I didn't. I did not. I——"

"Well, you were the last one who had a hold on it, and now it's gone. Now we need another rope. Of course, if you don't *care* about getting back . . . Or if you think you'll do better on your own . . ."

Eventually Neil agreed. "But Blossom ain't going to touch him, understand? She's my sister, and I ain't going to have it. *Understand?*"

"Neil, you don't have to worry about anything of that sort till we're all home safe," Buddy temporized. "Nobody's going to——"

"And they better not speak to each other either. Cause I say so, and what I say *goes*. Blossom, you go on ahead of me, and Buddy behind. Orville goes last."

Neil, naked now except for belt and holster, knotted the legs of their several trousers together, and they set off, each with a grip on the line. The water was deep and so hot their skin seemed to be coming off their bones, like a chicken that boils too long. The current was weakening, however, and they moved more slowly.

Soon they had found a root angling upward from which the trickle of water was not much worse than when they'd first noticed it—how many days ago? Wearily, almost mechanically, they began to climb again.

Blossom remembered a song from nursery school days about a spider washed down a water spout by the rain:

> Out came the sun and dried away the rain,
> And the inky-dinky spider be-*gan* to climb again.

She began to laugh, as she had laughed at the strange words of Jeremiah's poem, but this time she couldn't stop laughing, despite how much the laughter hurt.

Of them all, Buddy was the most upset by this, for he could remember the winter before, in the commonroom, and the people who had run out into the thawing snow, laughing and singing, never to return. Blossom's laughter was not unlike theirs.

The root at this point opened onto a tuber of fruit, and they decided to rest and eat. Orville tried to calm Blossom, but Neil told him to shut up. The pulp, which was now semi-liquid, dropped down on their heads and shoulders like the droppings of huge, diarrhetic birds.

Neil was torn between his desire to go away where the noise of his sister's laughter wouldn't disturb him and an equally strong desire to stay close at hand and protect her. He compromised, removing to a middle distance where he lay on his back, not intending to go to sleep, just to rest his body . . .

His head came down on the handle of the axe that Jeremiah had dropped there. He let out a little cry, which nobody noticed. They were all of them so tired. He sat for a long time, thinking very hard, his eyes crossing with the effort, though you couldn't see anything in that uncompromising dark.

The softened fruit pulp continued to fall from overhead and spatter on their bodies and on the floor with little crepitant sounds, like the sounds of children's kisses.

FIFTEEN **BLOOD AND LICORICE**

His hand touched her dead body. Buddy thought at first it was his father's corpse, but then he remembered how he had once already stumbled across that same cold body, and delight displaced terror: there *was* a way back! This was the thread that led out of the labyrinth. He traced his steps back to Orville and Blossom.

"Is Neil asleep?" he asked.

"He's stopped whistling," Orville said. "He's either asleep or dead."

Buddy told them his news. ". . . and so, you see, that means we can go back the way we tried to in the first place. Up the shaft. It was a mistake, our turning back when we did."

"Here we are, come full circle. The only difference now," Orville observed, "is that we've got Neil with us. Perhaps we'd do best to ignore that difference and leave him behind. We can go now."

"I thought we'd agreed to let the *others* decide what to do with Neil."

"We won't be doing away with him. We'll be leaving him in almost exactly the same place we found him—caught in the trap he meant for you. Besides, we can leave Alice's body in his way, and he can figure out for himself that the way back is up the shaft he threw her down."

"Not my half-brother. Not Neil. He'd only get scared if he found her body. As for figuring his way back, you might as well expect him to discover the Pythagorean theorem all by himself. Hell, I'll bet if you tried to explain that to him, he wouldn't believe it."

Blossom, who had been listening to all this rather dazedly, began to shiver, as the tension which her body had sustained so long began to drain away. It was like the time she'd gone swimming in the lake in April; her flesh trembled, yet at the same time she felt strangely rigid. Then her body, naked and taut, was suddenly pressed against Orville's, and she did not know if he had come to her or she to him. "Oh darling, we'll go back! We *will*—after all! Oh, my very own!"

Neil's voice shrilled in the darkness: "I heard that!"

Though she could hear Neil gallumphing forward, Blossom sustained the kiss desperately. Her fingers tightened into Orville's arms, grappled in the wiry muscles. Her body strained forward as his tried to pull away. Then a hand closed around her mouth and another around her shoulder and pulled her roughly away from Orville, but she didn't care. She was still giddy with the high, maenad happiness of those who are reckless in their love.

"I suppose you were giving him some more artificial respiration?" Neil sneered. It was, perhaps, his first authentic joke.

"I was kissing him," Blossom replied proudly. "We're in love."

"I forbid you to kiss him!" Neil screamed. "I forbid you to be in love. I forbid you!"

"Neil, let go of me." But his hands only shifted to secure a better grip and closed tighter.

"You, *you*—Jeremiah Orville! I'm going to *git* you. Yeah, I've been on to you right along. You fooled a lot of people, but you never fooled me. I knew what you was up to. I saw the way you looked at Blossom. Well, you ain't going to get her. What you're going to get is a bullet in your head."

"Neil, let go—you're hurting me."

"Neil," Buddy said in a low, reasoning tone, the tone one adopts with frightened animals, "that girl is your sister. You're talking like he stole your girl. She's your *sister*."

"She is not."

"What in hell do you mean by that?"

"I mean I don't care!"

"You filth."

"Orville, was that you? Why don't you come here, Orville? I ain't going to let Blossom go. You're going to have to come and rescue her. Orville?"

He jerked Blossom's arms behind her back and circled the slender wrists with his left hand. When she struggled, he twisted her arms up painfully or cuffed her with his free hand. When she seemed pacified, he unsnapped the leather flap of his holster and took out his Python, as one removes jewelry from a gift box, lovingly. "Come here, Orville, and git what I got for you."

"Be careful. He does have a gun," Buddy said. "He has father's."

Buddy's voice came more from the right than Neil had expected. He shifted his weight, but he wasn't really worried, because he had a gun and they didn't.

"I know," Orville said.

A little to the left. The space inside this tuber was long and narrow, too narrow for them to circle around to either side of him.

"I got something for you too, Buddy, if you think you're going to move in when your buddy's brains are blown out. I got me an axe." He chirruped an ugly laugh. "Hey! that's a joke: Buddy . . . buddy, get it?"

"Your jokes stink, Neil. If you want to improve your personality, you shouldn't make jokes."

"This is just between me and Orville, Buddy. You go away, or . . . or I'll chop your head off, that's what I'll do."

"Yeah? With what, with your big front teeth?"

"Buddy," Orville cautioned, "he *may* have the axe. I brought it down here with me." Fortunately no one thought to ask why.

"Neil, let *go* now. Let go or—or I'll never speak to you again. If you stop acting this way, we can all go right up and forget this happened."

"No, you don't understand, Blossom. You're not safe yet." His body leaned forward until his lips were touching her shoulders. They rested there a moment, uncertain what to do. Then his tongue began to lick away the fruit pulp with which her whole body was slimed. She managed not to scream.

"When you're safe, I'll let you go, I promise. Then you can be my queen. There'll be just the two of us and the whole world. We'll go to Florida, where it never snows, the two of us." He spoke with unnatural eloquence, for he had stopped thinking too closely about what he said, and the words left his lips uncensored by the faulty mechanisms of consciousness. It was another triumph for the primordial. "We'll lay on the beach, and you can sing songs while I whistle. But not yet, little lady. Not until you're safe. Soon."

Buddy and Orville seemed to have stopped moving forward. All was quiet except for the plops of the ripe fruit. Neil's blood surged with the raw delight that comes from inducing fear in another animal. *They're afraid of me!* he thought. *Afraid of my gun!* The weight of the pistol in his hand, the way his fingers curved around it, the way one of them pressed against the trigger, afforded him pleasure more richly gratifying than his lips had known touching his sister's body.

They *were* afraid of him. They could hear his hard breathing and Blossom's theatrical whimpering (which she maintained, like a foghorn, just so they might hear it and gauge their distance), and they hung back. They had too much contempt for Neil to be ready to risk their lives desperately against his. Surely there was some way to trick him—to make *him* take the gamble.

Perhaps, Buddy reasoned, if he became angry enough, he would do something foolish—squander his single bullet on a noise in the dark or at least loose his grip on Blossom, which must by now be wearying. "Neil," he whispered, "everybody knows about you. Alice told everyone what you did."

"Alice is dead," Neil scoffed.

"Her ghost," Buddy hissed. "Her ghost is down here looking for you. On account of what you did to her."

"Ah, that's a lot of hooey. I don't believe in no ghosts."

"And on account of what you did to Father. That was a terrible thing to do, Neil. He must be awful angry with you. He must be looking for you, too. And he won't need a lamp to find you with."

"I didn't do *nothing!*"

"Father knows better than that. Alice knows better, doesn't she? We all do. That's how you got the pistol, Neil. You killed him to get it. Killed your own father. How does it feel to do something like that? Tell us. What did he say at the very last moment?"

"Shut up! shut up! shut up!" When he heard Buddy begin to talk again, he set up the same shrill chant, backing away meanwhile from the voice that seemed to be drawing nearer to him.

Then it was quiet again, and that was worse. Neil began to fill the quiet with his own words: "I didn't kill him. Why would I want to do that? He loved me more than he loved anybody else, cause I was the one that always stuck by him. I never ran away, no matter how much I wanted to. We were pals, Dad and me. When he died——"

"When you *murdered* him——"

"That's right—when I murdered him, he said, 'Now you're the leader, Neil.' And he gave me his gun. 'That bullet's for Orville,' he says. 'Yes, Dad,' I said, 'I'll do anything you say.' We were always pals, Dad and me. I *had* to kill him, you can see that, can't you? Why, he would have married off Blossom to Orville. He said so. *'Dad,'* says I, 'you gotta understand—Orville ain't one of us!' Oh, I explained it very careful, but he just lay there and wouldn't say a thing. He was dead. But nobody else cared. Everybody hated him except me. We were pals, Dad and me. Pals."

It was evident, to Orville, that Buddy's stratagem was failing of its desired effect. Neil was past the point where he could be shaken. He was over the edge.

While Neil spoke, Orville moved forward, crouched, his right hand exploring the air before him, tentative as a mouse's whisker. If Neil had not been holding Blossom, or if he had not had a gun, it would have been a simple matter of running in low and tackling. Now it was necessary, for his own sake but more especially for Blossom's, either to disarm him or to make sure that his shot went wild.

To judge by his voice, Neil could not be far off. He swung his hand around in a slow arc, and it encountered not the gun, not Neil, but Blossom's thigh. She did not betray her surprise by the slightest flinch. Now it would be easy to wrench the gun from Neil's hand. Orville's hand stretched up and to the left; it should be right about *here.*

The metal of the gun barrel touched Orville's forehead. The weapon made such perfect contact that Orville could feel the hollow bore, concave within a distinct circlet of cool metal.

Neil pulled the trigger. There was a clicking sound. He pulled the trigger again. Nothing.

Days of immersion in the sap had effectually dampened the gunpowder.

Neil did not understand, then or ever, *why* the gun had failed him, but after another hollow *click,* he was aware that it had. Orville's fist came up for his solar plexus and glanced off his rib cage. As Neil toppled backward, the hand holding the pistol struck down with full force where he supposed Orville's head must be. The gunbutt struck against something hard. Orville made a noise.

Lucky—Neil was lucky. He struck down again and hit something soft. No noise. Orville's body was limp at his feet. Blossom had gotten away, but he didn't mind so much about that now.

He pulled out the axe from his gun belt, where it had been hanging, the head flat against his stomach, the handle crossing his left thigh.

"You stay away, Buddy, you hear? I still got me an axe."

Then he jumped on Orville's belly and his chest, but it was no good without shoes on, so he sat down on his belly and began hitting him in the face with his fists. Neil was beside himself. He laughed—oh, how he laughed!

But even so he stopped at intervals to take a few swipes at the darkness with the axe. "Whoop-pee!" he yelled. "Whoop-pee!"

Someone was screaming. Blossom.

The hard part was to keep Blossom from rushing right back into the thick of it. She just wouldn't listen.

"No!" Buddy said. "You'd get yourself killed. You don't know what to do. Listen—stop screaming and listen!" He shook her. She quieted. "I can get Orville away from him, so let *me* do it. Meanwhile, you go up the shaft the way we went before. Along the detour. Do you remember the way?"

"Yes." Dully.

"You'll do that?"

"Yes. But you've got to get Jeremiah away from him."

"Then I'll expect to see you up there. Go on now."

Buddy picked up Alice's rigid and festering corpse, which had been already in his hands when Orville had rushed in like a fool and spoiled everything. He lugged it a few feet in the direction of Neil's voice, stopped, grappled the old woman's body to his chest like a suit of armor. "Oooow," he moaned.

"Buddy," Neil shouted, standing, hoisting the axe, "you go away."

But Buddy only went on making the same silly moans and groans that children make playing ghost on a summer nigh or in a dark attic.

"You can't scare me," Neil said. "I ain't scared of the dark."

"It isn't me, I swear," Buddy said calmly. "it's Alice's ghost. She's coming to get you. Can't you tell by the smell it isn't me?"

"Ah, that's a lot of hooey," Neil retorted. The moaning started up again. He was uncertain whether to return to Orville or go after Buddy. "Stop it," he yelled, "I don't like that noise."

He could smell it! It was the way his father had smelled when he was dying!

Buddy's aim was good. The corpse struck Neil full-force across his body. A stiff hand grabbed at his eyes and wiped across his mouth, tearing his lip. He toppled, waving the axe wildly. The corpse made an awful screaming sound. Neil screamed too. Maybe it was just all one scream, Neil's and the corpse's together. Someone was trying to pull the axe away! Neil pulled back. He rolled over and over again and got to his feet. He still had the axe. He swung it.

Instead of Orville, there was someone else underneath his feet. He felt the rigid face, the long hair, the puffy arms. It was Alice. She wasn't tied, and the gag was out of her mouth.

Someone was screaming. Neil.

He screamed all the while he hacked apart the dead woman's body. The head came off with one stroke of the axe. He split the skull with another. Again and again he buried the axe head into her torso, but that wouldn't seem to come apart. Once the axe slipped and struck his ankle a glancing blow. He fell over, and the dismembered body squished under him like rotten fruit. He began to tear it to pieces with his hands. When there was no more possibility that it would haunt him again, he stood up, breathing heavily, and called out, not without a certain reverence: "Blossom?"

I'm right here.

Ah, he knew she would stay behind, he knew it! "And the others?" he asked.

They've gone away. They told me to go away too, but I didn't. I stayed behind.

"Why did you do that, Blossom?"

Because I love you.

"I love you too, Blossom. I always have. Since you were just a little kid."

I know. We'll go away together. Her voice singsonged, lulled him, rocked his tired mind like a cradle. *Someplace far away where nobody can find us. Florida. We'll live together, just the two of us, like Adam and Eve, and think of new names for all the animals.* Her voice grew stronger, clearer, and more beautiful. *We'll sail on a raft down the Mississippi. Just the two of us. Night and day.*

"Oh," said Neil, overcome with this vision. He began to walk toward the beautiful strong voice. "Oh, go on." He was walking in a circle.

I'll be the queen and you'll be my king, and there won't be anybody else in the world.

His hand touched her hand. His hand trembled.

Kiss me, she said. *Isn't that what you've always wanted?*

"Yes." His lips sought her lips. "Oh yes."

But her head, and therefore her lips, was not where one would have expected it to be. It was not attached to her neck. At last he found her head a few feet away. The lips that he kissed tasted of blood and licorice.

And for a few days, he satisfied the years' pent-up lusts on the head of Alice Nemerov, R.N.

SIXTEEN HOME SAFE

Sometimes distance is the best cure, and if you want to recuperate you keep on going. Besides, if you stopped, you couldn't be sure of starting up again. Not that they had that much choice—they *had* to keep going up. So they went up.

It was easier this time. Perhaps it was just the contrast between a sure thing (sure if they didn't slip, but that sort of danger hardly stimulated their adrenals at this point) and the distinct if unacknowledged presence of death that had burdened these last few days, so that their ascent was also a resurrection.

There was only one anxiety now, and it was Buddy's. Then even this was dissipated, for after less than an hour of climbing they had reached the level of their home base, and Maryann was waiting there. The lamp was burning so they could see again, and the sight of each other, mired as they were, bruised, bleeding, brought tears to their eyes and made them laugh like children at a birthday party. The baby was all right, they were all right, everything was all right.

"Do you want to go up to the surface now? Or do you want to rest?"

"Now," Buddy said.

"Rest," said Orville. He had just discovered that his nose was broken. It had always been such a good nose too—straight and thin, a proud nose. "Does it look awful?" he asked Blossom.

She shook her head sadly and kissed his nose, but she wouldn't say anything. She hadn't said a word since the thing that had happened down there. Orville tried to return her kiss, but she averted her head.

Buddy and Maryann went away so they could be by themselves. "He seems so much bigger," Buddy remarked, dandling Buddy Junior. "How long have we been gone?"

"Three days and three nights. They were long days, because I couldn't sleep. The others have already gone up to the surface. They wouldn't wait. But I knew you'd be back. You promised me. Remember?"

"Mmm," he said, and kissed her hand.

"Greta's come back," Maryann said.

"That makes no difference to me. Not any more."

"It was on your account that she came back. She told me so. She says she can't live without you."

"She's got her nerve—saying that to you."

"She's . . . changed. You'll see. She's not back in the same tuber where I was waiting, but in the one next above. Come, I'll bring you to her."

"You sound like you *want* me to take up with Greta again."

"I only want what you want, Buddy. You say that Neil is dead. If you want to make her your second wife, I won't stop you . . . if that's what you want."

"That's not what I want, dammit! And the next time I say I love you, you'd better believe me. Okay?"

"Okay," she said in her teensiest, church-mouse voice. There was even the suggestion of small laughter, stifled. "But you'd better see her anyhow. Because you'll have to think of some way of getting her back to the surface. Mae Stromberg is back too, but she's already gone up with the rest of them. She's sort of crazy now. She was still carrying her

Denny around with her—what's left of Denny. Bones mostly. This is the tuber. Greta's over at the other end. I'll stay back here with the lamp. She prefers the dark."

Buddy smelled a rat. Soon, advancing through the tuber, he smelled something much worse. Driving through a town in southern Minnesota in pea-canning season once, he had smelt something like this—an outhouse gone sour. "Greta?" he said.

"Buddy, is that you, Buddy?" It was surely her voice that replied, but its timbre had altered subtly. There was no crispness to the *d*'s, and the initial *B* had a sputtering sound. "How are you, Buddy? Don't come any closer than you are! I—" There was a gasping sound, and when Greta began to speak again, she burbled, like a child who tries to talk with his mouth full of milk. "—shill lub you. I wan oo be yours. Forgib me. We can begin all over again—like Adamb an Ebe—jus us oo."

"What's wrong with you?" he asked. "Are you sick?"

"No. I—" A sound of violent gargling. "—I'm just a little hungry. I get that way now and again. Maryann brings me my food here, but she won't ever bring me enough. Buddy, *she's trying to starve me!*"

"Maryann," Buddy called. "Bring the light here."

"No, don't!" Greta shouted. "You've got to answer my question first, Buddy. There's nothing standing between us now. Maryann told me that if you wanted—— No—go away! The light hurts my eyes." There was a slopping, sucking sound, as when one moves too suddenly in a full bathtub, and the air was roiled, releasing new tides of fetor.

Maryann handed her husband the dimly burning lamp, which he held over the sty into which the huge bulk of Greta Anderson had sunk of its own great weight. Her bloated body had lost any distinctively human features: it was an uncomplicated mass of flaccid fat. The contours of her face were obscured by folds of loose flesh like a watercolor portrait that has been left out of doors in a rainstorm. Now this face began to move from side to side, setting the flesh into a jellylike commotion—a gesture of negation, as far as one could judge.

"She doesn't move any more," Maryann explained, "and she's too heavy to lift. The others found her when they were looking for Blossom, and they pulled her this far with ropes. I told them to leave her here, cause she needs someone to look after her. I bring her all her food. It's a full-time job."

The commotion of flesh at their feet became more agitated, and there seemed almost to be an expression on the face. Hatred perhaps. Then an aperture opened in the center of the face, a mouth, and Greta's voice said, "Go away, you *disgush* me!"

Before they had left, the figure at their feet was already stuffing handfuls of the syrupy fruit pulp into the cavity in the center of its face.

While the men and Blossom rested, Maryann rigged a sort of harness and even succeeded, over loud protests, in cinching it about Greta. Maryann fetched another heaping portion of swill using the laundry basket that had been rescued from the common room fire. If this wasn't done for Greta at hourly intervals, she would begin to take up handfuls of the surrounding filth and stuff her gullet full of it. She no longer seemed to be aware of the difference, but Maryann was, and it was largely for her own sake that she kept the basket replenished. After Greta had downed sufficient of the fruit pulp, she was usually good, as now, for a few moments of conversation, and Maryann had been grateful for this during the long, dark hours of waiting. As Greta had often observed during these sober interludes: "The worst part is the boredom. That's what got me into my *condition*."

Now, however, she was pursuing a less weighty subject: "There was another movie, I can't remember the name now, where she was poor and had this funny accent, and Laurence Harvey was a medical student who fell in love with her. Or else it was Rock Hudson. She had him right in the palm of her hand, she did. He'd have done anything she said. I can't remember how that one ended, but there was another one I liked better, with James Stewart—remember him?—where she lived in this beautiful mansion in San Francisco. Oh, you should have seen the dresses she had. And such lovely hair! She must have been the most beautiful woman in the world. And she fell down from a tower at the end. I *think* that's how it ended."

"You must have seen just about every movie Kim Novak ever made," Maryann said placidly while the baby nursed at her breast.

"Well, if there was any I missed, I never heard about them. I wish you'd loosen these ropes." But Maryann never replied to her complaints. "There was one where she was a witch, but not, you know, old-fashioned. She had an apartment right on Park Avenue or someplace like that. And the most beautiful Siamese cat."

"Yes, I think you've told me about that one already."

"Well, why don't you ever contribute to the conversation? I must have told you about every movie I've ever seen by now."

"I never saw many movies."

"Do you suppose she's still alive?"

"Who—Kim Novak? No, I don't suppose so. We may be the very last ones. That's what Orville says."

"I'm hungry again."

"You just ate. Can't you wait till Buddy is finished nursing?"

"I'm *hungry,* I tell you! Do you think I *like* this?"

"Oh, all right." Maryann took up the basket by its one remaining handle and went off to a more wholesome section of the tuber. Filled, the basket weighed twenty pounds or more.

When she could no longer hear Maryann nearby, Greta burst out into tears. "Oh God, I *hate* this! I hate *her!* Oh, I'm so *hungry!*" Her tongue ached to be covered with the beloved, licorice-flavored slop, as a three-pack smoker's tongue craves nicotine on a morning when he has no cigarettes.

She was not able to wait for Maryann's return. When she had driven away the worst of her hunger, she stopped cramming the stuff in her mouth and moaned aloud in the darkness. "Oh Ga, how I hay myself! *Myself,* thas who I hay!"

They had hauled Greta a long way, only stopping to rest when they had reached the uppermost tuber in which they had spent the first night of their subterranean winter. The relative coolness at this height was a welcome relief from the steamy heat blow. Greta's silence was an even more welcome contrast. All during the ascent she had complained that the harness was strangling her, that she was caught in the vines and they were pulling her apart, that she was hungry. As they passed through each successive tuber, Greta would stuff the pulp into her mouth at a prodigious rate.

Orville estimated that she weighed four hundred pounds. "Oh, more than that," Buddy said. "You're being kind."

They would never have been able to get her as far as they had, if the sap coating the hollow of the roots had not been such an effective lubricant. The problem now was how to hoist her up the last thirty, vertical feet of the primary root. Buddy suggested a system of pulleys, but Orville feared that the ropes at their disposal might not be able to support Greta's full weight. "And even if they can how will we get her out through that hole? In December, Maryann was barely able to squeeze in through it."

"One of us will have to go back for the axe."

"Now? Not *this* one of us—not when we're this close to the sunlight. I say let's leave her here where there's food ready at hand for her and go up the rest of the way ourselves. Later is time enough to be Good Samaritans."

"Buddy, what's that sound?" Maryann asked. It was not like Maryann to interrupt.

They listened, and even before they heard it, they feared what it might be, what it was. A low grating sound—a whine—a rasp not so loud a noise as the metal sphere had made trying to push its way into the cave, because, for one thing, it was farther away, and for another, it did not seem to be having the same difficulty purchasing entrance. The whine grew louder; then a vast flushing sound ensued, as when a swimming pool begins to drain.

Whatever it was, it was now in the tuber with them.

With a fury sudden as their terror, a wind sprang up and bowled them to their knees. Tides of liquid fruit rose from the floor and walls and dropped from the ceiling; the wind swept off the crest of each successive wave and carried it toward the far end of the tuber, like the superfluous suds that spill out of an automatic washer. All that could be seen in the lamplight were white flashes of the blowing froth. Maryann clutched her child to her breast convulsively, after a blast of wind had almost lifted him from her arms. Assisted by Buddy, leaning into the wind, she made her way to the sanctuary of a root that branched off from the tuber. There they were sheltered from the worst effects of the gale, which seemed to howl still more fiercely now.

It was left to Orville to attempt Greta's rescue, but it was a hopeless task. Even under ordinary circumstances, it was difficult to pull her weight across the slippery floor of the fruit; alone, against the wind, he could not budge her. In fact, she seemed to be moving into the vortex with the pulp of the fruit. After a third quixotic attempt, he surrendered willingly to Blossom's mute entreaties and they joined Buddy and Maryann in the root.

Greta's ponderous weight slid forward with the other matter of the fruit. Miraculously, the lamp which had been entrusted to her during the rest period was still burning. Indeed it burned brighter than before.

Though her vision was beginning to flicker like badly spliced film, she was certain in the last moments of consciousness that she could see the great, palpitant maw of the thing, a brilliant rosy orange that could only be called Pango Peach and, superimposed over it, a grille of scintillating Cinderella Red. The grille seemed to grow at an alarming pace. Then she felt the whole mass of her being swept up in the whirlwind, and for a brief, weightless moment she was young again, and then she spattered over the grille like a cellophane bag of water dropped from a great height.

In the root they heard the popping sound distinctly. Maryann crossed herself, and Buddy mumbled something.

"What'd you say?" Orville shouted, for the tempest had reached its height, and even here in the root they were clinging to the vines to keep from being sucked back into the tuber.

"I said there'll be worms in the cider tonight," Buddy shouted back.

"What?"

"Worms!"

The rasping sound, which had ceased or been inaudible during the storm, was renewed, and as abruptly as the wind had sprung up, it died. When the rasping sounds had diminished to a reassuring level, the five of them returned to the tuber. Even without the lantern, the change was evident: the floor was several feet lower than it had been; voices echoed from the surfaces, which were hard as rock; even the thick rind of the fruit had been scraped loose. In the center of this larger space, at about the level of their heads, a large tube or pipeline stretched from the upper root opening to the lower. The tube was warm to the touch and was in constant movement—down.

"That was some vacuum cleaner," Orville said. "It scoured this place as clean as a whistle. There's not enough left here to feed a mouse."

"The harvesters have come," Buddy said. "You didn't think they'd plant all these potatoes and leave them to rot, did you?"

"Well, we better go up to the surface and see what Farmer Mac-Gregor looks like."

But they were strangely reluctant to leave the dry tuber. An elegiac mood had settled over them. "Poor Greta," Blossom said.

They all felt better when the simple memorial had been pronounced. Greta was dead, and the whole old world seemed to have died in her person. They knew that the world to which they would now ascend would not be the same as the one they'd left behind.

EPILOGUE THE EXTINCTION
OF THE SPECIES

Just as a worm passing through an apple may suppose that the apple, its substance and quality, consists merely of those few elements which have passed through his own meager body, while in fact his whole being is enveloped in the fruit and his passage has scarcely diminished it, so Buddy and Maryann and their child, Blossom and Orville, emerging from the earth after a long passage through the labyrinthine windings of their own, purely human evils, were not aware of the all-pervading presence of the larger evil that lies without, which we call reality. There is evil everywhere, but we can only see what is in front of our noses, only remember what has passed through our bellies.

The gray basketballs, pumped full of the pulp of the fruit, had risen from an earth that was no longer green. Then, like primitives clearing their lands, the machines that served the alien farmers turned that earth into a pyre. The towering stalks of the great Plants were consumed, and the sight had all the grandeur of a civilization falling to ruins. The few humans who remained retreated into the earth one more time. When they re-emerged, the pall that hung over the scorched earth made them welcome the total eclipse of night.

Then a wind moved in from the lake, and the pall thinned to reveal the heavy cumulus above. The rains came. The pure water cleared the skies and washed the months' encrustations from their bodies and soaked into the black earth.

Out came the sun and dried the rain, and their bodies gloried in its tenuous April warmth. Though the earth was black, the sky was blue, and at night there were stars—Deneb, Vega, Altair—brighter than anyone had remembered. Vega, particularly, shone bright. In the false dawn, a sliver of moon rose in the east. Later the sky would lighten, and once more the sun would rise.

It all seemed very beautiful to them, for they believed that the natural order of things—that is to say, their order—was being restored.

There were expeditions down into the roots to search out traces of fruit that the harvesters had overlooked. Such traces were rare, but they existed; by rationing out these scraps of rind sparingly, they might hope to survive the summer at least. For the time being, there was also the water and weeds in the lake, and as soon as it became warmer, they planned to make their way down along the Mississippi, to the warm southlands. There was also the hope that the ocean would still be fruitful.

The lake was dead. All along the fire-blackened shore, shoals of stinking fish were heaped memorially. But that the ocean might be in the same condition—that was unthinkable.

Their chief hope was that the Earth had survived. Somewhere there must be seeds sprouting in the warm soil, survivors like themselves, from whose flowering the earth might be made green again.

But their cardinal hope without which all hopes else were vain, was that the Plant had had its season, long though it had been, and that that season was over. The armored spheres had left with the rape of a planet, the fires had burnt over the stubble, and the land would now wake from the nightmare of that second alien creation. That was their hope.

Then everywhere the land was covered with a carpet of the richest green. The rains that had washed the sky clean of the smoke of the burning had also borne the billion spores of the second planting. Like all hybrids, the Plant was sterile, and could not reproduce itself. A new crop had to be planted every spring.

In two days the Plants were already ankle-deep.

The survivors spread out over the flat green uniformity of the plain resembled the figures in a Renaissance print illustrating the properties of perspective. The nearest three figures, in the middle distance, comprised a sort of Holy Family, though moving closer, one could not help but note that their features were touched by some other emotion than quiet happiness. The woman sitting on the ground was, in fact, weeping bitterly, and the man on his knees behind her, his hands planted on her shoulders as though to comfort her, was barely able to restrain his own tears. Their attention was fixed upon the thin child in her arms, who was futilely pulling at her dry breast.

A little farther on was another figure—or should we say two?— without any iconographic parallel, unless we allow this to be a Niobe sorrowing for her children. However, Niobe is usually depicted alone or in the prospect of all fourteen children; this woman was holding the skeleton of a single child in her arms. The child had been about ten years of age when it died. The woman's red hair was a shocking contrast to the green everywhere about her.

Almost at the horizon one could make out the figures of a man and woman, nude, hand in hand, smiling. Certainly these were Adam and Eve before the Fall, though they appeared rather more thin than they are usually represented. Also, they were rather ill-matched with respect to age: he was forty if he was a day; she was barely into her teens. They were walking south, and occasionally they would speak to each other.

The woman, for instance, might turn her head to the man and say, "You never told us who your favorite actor is." And the man would reply, "David Niven, I always liked David Niven." Then how beautifully they would smile!

But these figures were very, very small. The landscape dominated them entirely. It was green and level and it seemed of infinite extent. Vast though it was, Nature—or Art—had expended little imagination upon it. Even viewed closely, it presented a most monotonous aspect. In any square foot of ground, a hundred seedlings grew, each exactly like every other, none prepossessing.

Nature is prodigal. Of a hundred seedlings only one or two would survive; of a hundred species, only one or two.

Not, however, man.

Behold even to the moon, and it shineth not;
yea, the stars are not pure in his sight.

How much less man, that is a worm? and
the son of man, which is a worm?

Job 25:5–6

MARTIAN TIME-SLIP
by Philip K. Dick

On the arid colony of Mars the only thing more precious than water may be a ten-year-old schizophrenic boy named Manfred Steiner. For although the UN has slated "anomalous" children for deportation and destruction, other people—especially Supreme Goodmember Arnie Kolt—suspect that Manfred's disorder may be a window into the future.

Science Fiction/0-679-76167-5

VIRTUAL UNREALITIES
The Short Fiction of Alfred Bester
with an Introduction by Robert Silverberg

Alfred Bester took science fiction into hyperdrive, endowing it with a wit, speed, and narrative inventiveness that have inspired two generations of writers. Read about the sweet-natured young man whose phenomenal good luck turns out to be disastrous for the rest of humanity. Meet a warlock who practices on Park Avenue, or make a deal with the devil—but not without calling your agent. *Virtual Unrealities* is a historic collection from one of science fiction's true pathbreakers.

A Vintage Original
Science Fiction/0-679-76783-5

EXEGESIS
by Astro Teller

"I request mail. I am edgar. I explore." Meet edgar. He's very smart, though sometimes a bit naive. edgar has a great sense of humor, though sometimes a bit on the wild side. edgar is an artificial intelligence computer program invented by Alice Wu at her lab in Stanford, where it becomes apparent that not only is edgar real, but completely beyond Alice's—or anyone else's—control.

A Vintage Contemporaries Original
Fiction/0-375-70051-X

ALSO BY THOMAS M. DISCH

CAMP CONCENTRATION

In this chillingly plausible work of speculative fiction, Thomas M. Disch imagines an alternate 1970s in which America has declared war on the rest of the world—and much of its own citizenry—and is willing to use any weapon to assure victory, even an "intelligence maximization" drug that is also invariably fatal.

"It is a work of art, if you read it, you will be changed."
—Ursula K. LeGuin
Science Fiction/0-375-70545-7

334

Thomas M. Disch portrays life on the social and economic margins of 21st-century New York. As Disch charts the intricate and baroquely dysfunctional relationships among the residents of the public housing project at 334 East 11th Street, he immerses readers in a world as grimly authentic as Dickens's London—where babies are rationed, drugs are licensed, real food is displayed in museums, and hospital attendants moonlight as bodysnatchers.

"A work to stand with the best American fiction of the 70s."
—Jonathan Lethem, *The Village Voice Literary Supplement*
Science Fiction/0-375-70544-9

Printed in the United States
by Baker & Taylor Publisher Services